Sky couldn't help it if it sounded like an accusation.

"You heard," Meredith calmly replied.

That was it? That was all she had to say? "Are you going to tell me who the father is?"

"In the past four years I've only been with one man." While the implication was still soaking in, she moved backward, stepping inside the shop. "But don't worry, I wouldn't marry you if you were the last man on earth."

Then the door slammed. And Sky blinked. The lock clicked into place.

She wouldn't marry him if he were the last man on earth? Who'd said anything about marriage? Besides, *if* he set his mind on marrying a woman, she darn well would be his wife!

Dear Reader,

This holiday season, as our anniversary year draws to a close, we have much to celebrate. The talented authors who have published—and continue to publish—unforgettable love stories. You, the readers, who have made our twenty-year milestone possible. And this month's very special offerings.

First stop: BACHELOR GULCH, Sandra Steffen's popular ongoing miniseries. They'd shared an amazing night together; now a beguiling stranger was back in his life carrying *Sky's Pride and Joy*. She'd dreamed *Hunter's Vow* would be the marrying kind...until he learned about their child he'd never known existed—don't miss this keeper by Susan Meier! Carolyn Zane's BRUBAKER BRIDES are back! *Montana's Feisty Cowgirl* thought she could pass as just another *male* ranch hand, but Montana wouldn't rest till he knew her secrets...and made this 100% woman completely his!

Donna Clayton's SINGLE DOCTOR DADS return...STAT. *Rachel and the M.D.* were office assistant and employer...so why was she imagining herself this widower's bride and his triplets' mother? Diana Whitney brings her adorable STORK EXPRESS series from Special Edition into Romance with the delightful story of what happens when *Mixing Business...with Baby*. And debut author Belinda Barnes tells the charming tale of a jilted groom who finds himself all dressed up...to deliver a pregnant beauty's baby—don't miss *His Special Delivery!*

Thank you for celebrating our 20th anniversary. In 2001 we'll have even more excitement—the return of ROYALLY WED and Marie Ferrarella's 100th book, to name a couple!

Happy reading!

Mary-Theresa Hussey

Mary-Theresa Hussey
Senior Editor

Please address questions and book requests to:
Silhouette Reader Service
U.S.: 3010 Walden Ave., P.O. Box 1325, Buffalo, NY 14269
Canadian: P.O. Box 609, Fort Erie, Ont. L2A 5X3

Sky's Pride and Joy

SANDRA STEFFEN

SILHOUETTE *Romance*

Published by Silhouette Books

America's Publisher of Contemporary Romance

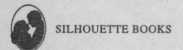 SILHOUETTE BOOKS

ISBN 0-373-19486-2

SKY'S PRIDE AND JOY

Copyright © 2000 by Sandra E. Steffen

Visit Silhouette at www.eHarlequin.com

Printed In U.S.A.

Books by Sandra Steffen

SANDRA STEFFEN

Growing up the fourth child of ten, Sandra developed a keen appreciation for laughter and argument. Sandra lives in Michigan with her husband, three of their sons and a blue-eyed mutt who thinks her name is No-Molly-No. Sandra's book *Child of Her Dreams* won the 1994 National Readers' Choice Award. Several of her titles have appeared on the national bestseller lists.

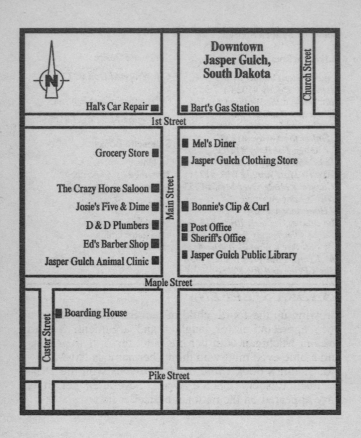

Downtown Jasper Gulch, South Dakota

N

Church Street

Hal's Car Repair ■ ■ Bart's Gas Station

1st Street

Grocery Store ■ ■ Mel's Diner
■ Jasper Gulch Clothing Store

The Crazy Horse Saloon ■

Main Street

Josie's Five & Dime ■ ■ Bonnie's Clip & Curl

D & D Plumbers ■ ■ Post Office
■ Sheriff's Office
Ed's Barber Shop ■

Jasper Gulch Animal Clinic ■ ■ Jasper Gulch Public Library

Maple Street

Custer Street

■ Boarding House

Pike Street

Chapter One

Skyler Buchanan hoisted the last fifty-pound sack of feed onto his shoulder and headed for his truck. Neil Anderson, manager of the J.P. Feed and Ranch Supply Store, wrestled the sack from Sky's shoulder, adding it to the top of the stack on the bed of the truck before climbing morosely to the ground. "Gonna be another scorcher, that's for sure."

Sky cast a cursory glance at the horizon. The sky was clear, the midmorning sun hot, the day promising to be hotter. Sky didn't mind the heat.

"Jake expectin' you back right away?" Norbert, the oldest Anderson brother, asked from the shade of the old building. The J.P. Feed & Ranch Supply Store sat around the corner from the village main street. The old-timers said it had been painted once, but nobody could agree on the year, or the color. Whatever color it had once been, time had dulled it to the same faded, weathered gray of all three of the Anderson brothers' cowboy hats.

At Sky's shrug, Norbert grimaced. "Oh, yeah. You

come and go as you please. I knew that. Must be this
heat."

"Either that," Ned, the middle brother added, "or boredom."

"God, yes," Neil declared. "Boredom. Not a dang
thing ever changes in this dusty corner of South Dakota."

Sky swiped his brown Stetson off his head, but again,
he only shrugged. Unlike the other bachelors in the area,
he wasn't looking for things to change around here. What
was wrong with life just the way it was? Besides, no matter
what the local boys said, not everything stayed the same
in Jasper Gulch. Babies were born, kids grew up, girls left
town, old folks died. There'd been other changes, too. New
stores had opened, a couple of businesses had changed
hands. In fact, one of those changes involved Neil, who'd
left the family ranch to manage the feed store a couple of
months back. Neil did a good job, but he still wasn't
happy. None of the Anderson brothers were. According to
the Jasper Gulch grapevine, Ned and Norbert spent so
much time here that folks had taken to wondering who
was minding the ranch.

"Grab yourself a root beer out of the cooler in the office
and sit a spell with us in the shade," Neil insisted.

Sky glanced at the other two men who were already
popping the tops of their soda cans. He could have taken
the time to join them, but he just wasn't in the mood to
listen to complaints about the weather and taxes and the
sorry price of beef and how nothing ever happened in Jasper Gulch. Cramming his hat back on his head, he said,
"Maybe next time, boys."

Without a backward glance, he climbed into his truck
and turned the key. The air streaming in his open window
was hot and dry. He considered stopping at the diner, settling at a quiet table, and ordering up a tall glass of lem-

onade or iced tea. He had plenty of time to make up his mind, because when he turned onto Main Street, he had to crawl to a stop in order to let the clucking hens otherwise known as the staunchest members of the Ladies Aid Society cross the street in front of him. He'd gotten on their good side a couple of years back when he'd sided with them instead of with the local boys who'd decided to advertise for women to come to their fair town. The leaders of the Society had insisted that such an ad would draw riffraff and worse, women of ill repute. Sky's reasons had been a lot less political.

As far as Sky was concerned, new women meant new problems. After all, the local gals knew better than to try to cage him in. He hadn't been so sure new women would be as easy to dissuade. As it turned out, only a handful of women had answered the ad. Much to the Society's relief, none of them had been ladies of the night. Much to his relief, it hadn't been all that difficult to convince most of the new gals that he wasn't the marrying kind. Once, he'd overheard DoraLee Brown talking to the Southern gal who hadn't figured it out on her own.

"Sugar," DoraLee had said, "Sky Buchanan is one of those men who can be civilized, but never tamed. He's easy on the eyes, but hard on the heart."

Keeping a safe distance from one of the local women and her young daughter who were crossing the street in front of him, Sky couldn't argue with DoraLee's logic. He didn't take credit for his looks or blame for his attitude. According to his mother, both had come straight from his old man, along with every shortcoming and flaw he possessed. Not that his mother had been any better. Which was why Skyler Buchanan was footloose and fancy-free, and planned to stay that way.

He lifted his hand to the old men shooting the breeze

in front of the barbershop, and at Cletus McCully who was sitting on the bench in his usual spot in front of the post office. They all waved in return in their usual way, Cletus without unhooking his thumb from his suspenders, Karl Hanson with his customary salute, Roy Everts with his arthritic hands that resembled hams. Unlike most folks in and around Jasper Gulch, Sky hadn't been born and raised here, but he'd been here so long that people had either forgotten or didn't care.

Sky never forgot where he'd spent the first seventeen years of his life. Oh, he'd had a roof over his head, and sometimes there had been food on the table. His upbringing pretty much ended there. He'd learned the difference between right and wrong on his own. He didn't kill, maim, swindle, lie or cheat. He put in an honest day's work in return for an honest day's pay, and he came and went as he pleased. He'd learned to deal with loneliness before he could talk. He'd learned to deal with desire years later. Except for a chance encounter with a leggy blonde a month ago, he's been as celibate as old Cletus McCully.

The image of hair the color of spun gold and a smile warm and soft enough to slice clear through a man's defenses wafted across Sky's mind. Damn, he'd been trying not to think about that leggy blonde or her soft smiles and gentle touch and... Clamping his mouth shut, he swore to himself.

He'd had no intention of sleeping with a woman he'd only just met, but something had been in the air that night. He didn't know what it was, but the same thing had been in Meredith Warner's gaze, as in his. Later, it had scared the spit right out of him, because it was damned close to need. At the time, he hadn't taken the time to analyze. Hell, he hadn't taken the trouble to think. Oh, but he'd taken the time to touch, and whisper, and feel and...

The sudden catch in his breathing, and the telltale hitch elsewhere reminded him of things he preferred not to think about, and made him hotter than the dusty air streaming through his open window. That had been happening a lot lately.

That did it. Forget iced tea. He was going to the Crazy Horse for a beer even if it was a little early in the day. He gave the street a sweeping glance in preparation to make a U-turn in front of the Saloon. A serious mistake. Not the U-turn. He never got around to making that. The serious mistake involved a glance at the women talking in front of an old building across the street from the Five & Dime. One of those women had long legs and shimmering blond hair. She turned her head, her gaze meeting his. A zing went through him, and he couldn't look away.

A horn blared. Sky swerved, missing Hal Everts' truck by less than a foot. The close call didn't alleviate the awareness that was buzzing through him. All because Meredith Warner was back in town.

A month ago, Sky had thought her stay here was temporary. That had made her safe. He'd heard she was coming back for good. Nothing like that could escape the Jasper Gulch grapevine. There she was, standing in front of a building that had been vacant for years, her hair hanging long and straight down her back, skin the color of peaches-and-cream, arms and ankles bare, every movement fluid. He couldn't see the color of her eyes from here, but he knew they were a deep, dark brown. It was unusual to come across a woman with hair so blond and eyes so dark, but she'd been a natural blonde, all right. He couldn't seem to forget the moment he'd discovered that particular fact.

Sky swore under his breath again, tore his gaze away from hers, and yelled an apology to Hal. Keeping his foot steady on the gas pedal and his eyes straight ahead, he drove out of town.

Now there's a man I'd steer clear of if I were you…"

Meredith had to give herself a mental shake in order to drag her gaze away from the dusty pickup truck rounding the corner at the end of Main Street. Bringing her attention back to Jayne Stryker, who had turned out to be a godsend, not to mention a genius when it came to advertising, Meredith wondered why someone couldn't have warned her a month ago.

It was too late for that. Besides, she'd promised herself there would be no more self-recriminations, no more looking back, no more wishing things could be different. She was still reeling from the reality that her only sister and brother-in-law had died as a result of a horrible car accident. Except for her young niece and nephew, she was completely alone in the world, but in many ways, she had been for years. The opening of the antiques and home furnishings store would mark a new beginning for Meredith. She was getting on with her life, and getting her life in order. It was too late to reconcile with Kate, but it wasn't too late to have a loving relationship with Kate's children, Logan and Olivia. Meredith was nearly thirty years old. From now on, she was going to make the right choices, do the right things. She was putting down roots. She would be a true friend to her new friends, and she would be the best aunt her niece and nephew could ask for.

"His name is Skyler Buchanan," Jayne Stryker added. "Rumor has it he's broken the hearts of nearly every girl in town. He's a complicated man. But then, aren't they all?"

Meredith eyed her newest and most interesting friend. She'd heard other women claim that men were simple. As far as Meredith was concerned, nothing was simple, least of all men. Evidently, Jayne felt the same way. Jayne Kincaid had come to Jasper Gulch last Christmas to visit her brother, Burke, who'd set up his medical practice here. She'd had no intention of staying. An ex-rodeo champion named Wes Stryker, who had happened to be Kate's and Dusty's best friend, had changed her mind, along with her plans for the future. Now, Jayne and Wes were raising Logan and Olivia. From what Meredith could see, they were doing an admirable job, too. Not that Logan and Olivia always made things easy. Which brought her back to the fact that nothing was easy.

"Meredith?"

Ah, yes, Meredith and Jayne were in total agreement when it came to their philosophies on life. Life had a way of getting complicated.

"Meredith?"

Throw in a man, and it usually spiraled out of control. That's what had happened that night a month ago. She'd been rocked clear to her soul from the news that Kate and Dusty had died. In had walked Skyler Buchanan. Their eyes had met, and a tornado might as well have swept everybody and everything else away, leaving the two of them in its center to ride out the storm. That storm had turned out to be an idyllic interlude unlike anything she'd ever experienced. She'd been foolish enough to believe, for those few brief hours, that it had been the same for him. She'd been wrong, of course. But she'd tried to put it out of her mind.

She'd known she would see Skyler Buchanan again. Which made forgetting the night she'd spent in his arms even more impossible to do.

"Earth to Meredith."

What? Oh. "Yes, Jayne?"

"Are you sure you want to keep Logan and Olivia with you while I attend this business lunch this afternoon?"

The area surrounding Meredith's heart swelled with gratitude. Jayne knew how much Meredith loved her only niece and nephew, and this was her way of giving Meredith an opportunity to spend time with the children. "Of course I'm sure. You said yourself it'll only be for an hour. Besides, I'm looking forward to it."

Jayne's careful perusal made Meredith feel like a fly under a microscope. It was a relief when Jayne turned her attention to the lanky cowboy sauntering toward them, a ten-year-old boy on one side, a five-year-old girl on the other. The first time Meredith had seen the children with Wes and Jayne Stryker, instead of with their parents, Kate and Dusty, she'd felt as if a knife had twisted in her heart. But the ache lessened each time she saw them. The kids were happy, and well adjusted. Meredith knew that Wes and Jayne had been worried that she, the children's closest living relative, might want to take them away. Meredith had put their minds at ease, for she didn't want to disrupt Logan's and Olivia's lives further. She only wanted to be near them, to get to know them, and to love them.

"Hi, Aunt Meredith," Logan called.

"Aunt Meredith, look!" Olivia held up a bedraggled stuffed goose. "Jaynie asked Kelsey's mama to give Snuggles new eyes, and she did. Now Snuggles is as good as new."

"Snuggles isn't either as good as new," Logan grumbled.

"Is so."

"Is not."

"Is so."

"Uh-uh."

"Uh-huh."

Jayne tucked a strand of short, dark hair behind her ear and glanced from her husband to Meredith. With a wink, she said, ''Unless you keep them busy, this could still be going on when I return. Burke and I used to be like that.''

''Kate and I did, too.''

''Then you'll know exactly how to deal with them,'' Jayne said.

''Forget child labor laws,'' Wes Stryker said, a twinkle in his blue eyes. ''Put them to work. There's nothing like manual labor to work out a kid's frustrations.'' He turned to the children. ''We'll be back in an hour, so try to be good. And you,'' he said, easing closer to his wife.

Meredith thought she heard Jayne whisper, ''I'll be good later.''

And she was pretty sure Wes said, ''I'm counting on it,'' the moment before his lips brushed his wife's.

The underlying sensuality went right over the children's heads. Tucking the stuffed goose under one arm, Olivia skipped into the store ahead of her brother. Knowing what could happen when those two were left unsupervised, Meredith hurried after them.

''Logan,'' she said, handing the boy the keys while she flipped on lights. ''Unlock the back door, would you? Maybe we can get a breeze blowing through here.''

Logan ran to the back of the store, keys jangling, shoes thudding, anything not anchored down rattling as if during an earthquake. Within seconds, the netting hanging from the rafters ruffled, a dozen sets of wind chimes purled, and Meredith sighed. Turning in a circle, she took it all in. She'd put everything she had into this store, all her energy and her life savings. She'd looked at several buildings, but had decided on the store that sat by itself between the Jasper Gulch Clothing Store and Bonnie's Clip & Curl. It had been nothing but a deserted building then, so full of cobwebs that she'd had the place fumigated before she'd done anything else. Some of the other structures she'd looked at had more history, but none of them had as much personality or potential.

The front portion of the store had a tin ceiling. The rest had an open ceiling, high rafters, and wood floors. A long time ago, it had been a furniture store, which made it the perfect place to house the antiques and fine furnishings Meredith planned to sell here. The work was nearly completed. Track lighting had been installed below the rafters, the entire place scrubbed and painted. She'd made the curtains at the windows herself, and with the help of several local teenagers, the antiques were arranged at one end, the few pieces of new furniture she could afford to stock at the other. The paint she would sell was due to arrive later in the week. Every day she worked from dawn until late into the night down here before retiring to the tiny apartment upstairs. It was all coming together, the kids, her store, her life.

She spread her arms wide and tipped her head back. Whoa. Woozy, she closed her eyes.

"Aunt Meredith, 'Livia," Logan called. "That alley cat's gone and had kittens in an old barrel that tipped over back here."

Olivia ran to see. Meredith blinked, focused, then followed. Logan was on his knees just inside the back door. Olivia was bent at the waist a foot away.

"She must'a just had 'em," he said. "They're still ugly and their eyes aren't open yet."

"They're not either ugly," Olivia exclaimed. "They're beautiful."

Meredith braced herself for the argument that was sure to break out, but Logan shrugged good-naturedly and simply said, "You know what I mean."

"How many are there?" Olivia asked her big brother.

"Six."

"Six?" Meredith exclaimed. What on earth was she going to do with an alley cat and six kittens?

"Wait. I was wrong."

Oh, good.

"There are seven," Logan amended.

"Seven?" Meredith asked. "Are you sure?" The scraggly orange-and-white mother cat stared up at her, blinking tiredly, as if sharing Meredith's dismay.

"Yup. There are seven all right. Uncle Wes says seven's lucky."

"We're lucky!" Olivia exclaimed. "Aren't we Aunt Meredith?"

Meredith took a closer look at that cat and her seven kittens, and then at the brown-haired children whose blue eyes, so like their mother's, were wide with wonder. A lump came and went in her throat, but she managed a small nod and a genuine smile.

"Seven kitties," Olivia declared. "Plus the mama. We're gonna need a lot of names."

Since Meredith knew that a named cat was a claimed cat, she had to think fast. "Those kittens need to take a nap right now. If you two want to think of names, why don't you help me decide what to call the store?"

"You want us to name a building?" Logan asked in that preadolescent, know-it-all attitude universal to males.

Meredith swiped a finger along his nose and said, "Not the building, silly. It's going to be my business, a way of life, an entity with its own unique personality."

The kids looked up at her blankly for a full five seconds before turning their gazes on each other. "I think we should name the white-and-yellow one Fluffy," Olivia said.

"And the one with the two white paws is..."

"Paws?" Olivia asked.

"No, silly. Boots."

Meredith knew when she'd been beaten. Retracing her footsteps to the front of the store, she began arranging throw pillows and lamps and candles on shelves lining one wall. The kids spent the next hour pondering names for kittens Meredith couldn't possibly keep. Logan made a bed for them in an old drawer he found in the back alley, and he and Olivia coaxed the mother to let him help her move the kittens to what they considered a better lodging place. As far as Meredith was concerned, those two voices were more musical than the resonant purl of the wind chimes swaying overhead in the gentle breeze.

By the time Jayne was due back to pick up the children an hour later, all the kittens had been duly petted and examined for any unusual, interesting or identifying markings, three of them had names, and Logan and Olivia were arguing over a fourth. Mercy, those kids could argue over nothing.

"You can't name the mother cat Haley!" Logan exclaimed.

"I can name her Haley if I want to!" Olivia declared with equal exuberance.

"Can not."

"Can so."

"You can't either name her Haley. That's a real person's name. Tell her Aunt Meredith."

Before Meredith could open her mouth, Olivia said, "We named the barn cats Carolyn, Sherilyn and Tom, and those are real people names. You just don't wanna name this one Haley on accounta you kissed Haley Carson and she gave you a black eye."

All at once, the store was absolutely quiet. Logan was

the quietest of all. Wanting to help but not sure how, Meredith said, "Olivia, you don't know that's the reason Logan doesn't want to name this cat Haley. I don't really think she looks like a Haley, do you? Besides, kissing is private."

"Kissing's icky," Olivia said. "Do you think kissing's icky, Aunt Meredith?"

Two pairs of trusting blue eyes turned to her. Kissing? "Well, er, um. That is…"

The bell over the front door jangled, signaling Jayne's return. Meredith was saved from having to try to come up with an answer that wasn't mostly a sigh. Icky? Oh, that depended upon who a woman kissed. And the last man, the only man she'd kissed in a long, long time, hadn't been icky at all.

Jayne dashed in long enough to pay due respect to the mother cat and her kittens, recount the high points of the meeting she'd attended, and say, "I'll see you at the town council meeting tonight!" before bustling the kids away.

Ugh, Meredith thought when she was alone again in the store. Tonight, at the town council meeting, she would have to stand in front of the women of the Ladies Aid Society and several of the bachelors in town. She prayed she passed everyone's scrutiny so that she might be accepted in this small town.

That was what she wanted. To be accepted, to be near Logan and Olivia, and for her store to be a success. In order for her store to be a success, she couldn't afford to make any enemies or hurt any feelings, which meant she had to let the overeager bachelors down gently, which wasn't easy to do when she received requests for dates every day. She could hardly blame them. There simply weren't enough women to go around out here. An old copy of the advertisement the local boys had put in the local papers to lure women to Jasper Gulch still hung in the post office and in the diner. Not a lot had changed since then. As far as Meredith could tell, in the three years since the ad had appeared, there wasn't a single man in town who wasn't still shy but willing. She paused for a moment.

That wasn't true. There was one. Oh, Skyler Buchanan had been more than willing a month ago, and she doubted he'd ever been shy.

Giving herself a mental shake, Meredith got back to work. It was amazing how many times her thoughts strayed to Sky, and a kiss, that had led to a touch, that had led to a frenzy of hands reaching, and buttons popping and clothes being peeled away like layers until so much more than two bodies were bared. For those few brief hours, Meredith had believed she'd been able to see into Sky's soul, and he into hers. Of course, when it was all over, they'd both known it had been a mistake. Skyler Buchanan was a free spirit, and Meredith Warner had an old soul. They'd both been lonely, that was all. Loneliness could be a powerful motivation, but not a basis for anything deep and abiding. Sky had been the first to put it into words, saying it would be best to end it then and there.

She'd nodded, mumbling her agreement, her clothes clutched in her arms, covering her nakedness as she'd assured him that there was nothing to end. In order for something to have an ending, it had to have a beginning. And all she and Sky had had were a few brief hours in each other's arms, a few brief hours during which two people had taken a respite from their real lives and had lived a fantasy.

She hadn't seen Sky since that night. Until today. She'd thought about him a thousand times. Which was just about how often she'd told herself to forget him, because surely, he hadn't given her another thought.

She'd been sure of that, until earlier, when their gazes had locked from a distance. Something powerful had passed between them. She wasn't sure what it was, but she found herself wondering if perhaps he was having a difficult time forgetting her, too.

She straightened fast, and got light-headed and woozy again. She eyed the sofas waiting for someone to buy them, wishing she could curl up on one of them, and close her eyes if only for a few minutes. Shaking her head slightly to clear it, she reminded herself that she didn't have time for the luxury of a nap. She had a business to launch, and a life to turn around. Placing a hand to the flat of her stomach, she hoped she wasn't coming down with the flu.

Chapter Two

"Hey, Sky." Neil Anderson slipped into one of the last vacant chairs in the room. "It's been a while since I've seen you at one of these meetings."

What could Sky say? He didn't attend town meetings often. Folks assumed he didn't like schedules or agendas, especially other people's. Nobody had ever thought to ask if he had some other reason. Tonight, he was here because his boss, Jake McKenna, who also happened to be his best friend as well as an exasperating man, had roped Sky into attending in his place.

Neil said, "You must have heard that Jayne Stryker's gonna introduce the new gal at the meeting, too, eh?"

Sky's eyebrows rose. Meredith was going to be here tonight? It certainly explained why the back room of Mel's Diner was busting at the seams, and a good share of Jasper Gulch's single men and a few married ones, as well, were balancing their cowboy hats on one knee.

Jake was going to owe him, big time.

Sky settled his shoulders more comfortably along the

back of the old folding chair, and left his Stetson on his head where it belonged. For the sake of idle curiosity and the general heck of it, he glanced around. He recognized every face present, but he didn't see Meredith.

Luke Carson banged his gavel on the table, calling the meeting to order. He, his brother, Clayt, and their friend, Wyatt McCully, had been instrumental in placing the original ad in the local papers luring women to Jasper Gulch. All three of them were married now, Luke and Wyatt to the first two women who'd moved here, and Clayt, to Jasper Gulch's own Melody McCully. The remaining sixty-some bachelors had done a lot of bellyaching about that, but then, a lot of those local boys did a lot of bellyaching about just about everything.

The meeting went surprisingly fast. It wasn't because the fine folks of Jasper Gulch were especially agreeable tonight. Sky had seen more than one man's face turn red beneath the tan line where a dusty Stetson normally sat. They were on their best behavior. Sky suspected it had to do with their readiness to bring on the main attraction.

He wondered what they would do if the rumor that Meredith was going to be here tonight turned out to be false. Sky happened to glance over his shoulder. The meeting went on around him, but he didn't participate. The Jasper Gulch grapevine was batting a thousand, as usual. Meredith stood near the door, looking straight ahead, her throat convulsing as if she were nervous. It was strange, because his first impression of her hadn't been of a shy woman. His first impression had been of an enchantress who knew her own mind, what she liked and what she wanted. She'd wanted him. Being wanted by a woman like her had been a heady sensation. A dangerous, heady sensation.

Luke pounded the table with his gavel again. "Before

we adjourn, Jayne Stryker has somebody she'd like you all to meet.''

"Finally."

"It's about time."

"I'll say."

Chairs creaked as the majority of the men sat up straighter. A few hardy paunches were sucked in, belts were adjusted, and everyone generally tried hard to look casual. As far as Sky was concerned, they tried a little too hard.

Jayne strolled to the front of the room. The woman had a walk that could stop traffic and a mouth that could, and had, singed the hairs of a good many of the local boys' ears. "Folks," she said, smiling wryly, fully aware that her quick wit and business savvy were exactly what this town needed. "It's nice to see so many people who care about their community." And then she launched into a lengthy update on the progress she was making setting up a mail-order catalog business in the old five-and-dime building. The members of the Ladies Aid Society listened with rapt attention. The boys fidgeted like the congregation on Palm Sunday.

Sky glanced at Meredith, and saw that she was shaking her head and smiling at Jayne as if they shared a private joke. With a wink and a slight movement of her head that prompted Meredith to stroll toward the front of the room, Jayne said, "Everybody, this is Meredith Warner, Logan and Olivia's aunt. I'm sure all of you have heard she's opening an antique slash furniture store in town. I invited her to stop by tonight to tell you a little about it. I hope you don't mind staying a few minutes longer."

Mind? It was what the men were here for.

Meredith turned to face the crowd. She wet her lips, a

serious mistake, unless it had been her intention to jump-start the men's fantasies.

"As Jayne said, I'm nearly ready to open my furniture, antiques and home furnishings store two doors down. I'm excited about that, but to tell you the truth, standing up here talking about it makes me nervous."

"Imagine us naked," one of the younger bachelors murmured just loud enough for her to hear.

"Oh, no," she said, staring Ben Jacobs down. "I'm not going there. Nobody is going to imagine anybody naked."

She glanced around the room sternly, as if to make her point. Sky wondered if he'd imagined that her gaze had settled on him for an instant longer than on anybody else. He wasn't imagining the change in the beating rhythm of his heart.

"As I was saying. I've worked in several different fields in order to make ends meet over the years. That's the funny thing about not knowing what you want to be when you grow up. You learn a lot about life and hone a lot of different skills in your quest to find your niche. Until moving here, I spent four years working as an interior designer for a large store in Minneapolis. Before that I was a seamstress, an upholsterer and a painter—of houses, not art—although to me, every house is its own work of art."

So, Sky thought, she was a midwesterner. That explained her accent. He wondered where she'd acquired her class, because that kind of poise didn't come from any one place or from doing odd jobs like sewing or painting.

The fan in the corner stirred her hair. There wasn't a man in the room who wasn't mesmerized by the movement of those silky tresses, the style of her trim, ankle-length skirt, and the fit of her sleeveless blouse. And no matter what she said, Sky doubted there was a man in the place who wasn't imagining what she would look like out of it.

She wasn't buxom, but she had curves in all the right places, curves he'd memorized with his hands, and lips and…

"…and I'm hoping to hire an apprentice or two to help me with the reupholstering and sewing."

Chairs creaked as a dozen hands shot into the air. The sudden hubbub drew Sky from his daydream.

Meredith had relaxed, as if enjoying the easy camaraderie with the people of Jasper Gulch. "Sorry," she said. "I'd prefer to interview women."

"Now ain't that a little prejudiced?" Ben Jacobs asked playfully.

"Mertyl?" Jayne Stryker sputtered, stepping closer to Meredith. "Raise two fingers like this." When the little gray-haired lady had done so, Jayne said, "Now whack Ben upside the head with them for me, would you, please?"

There was a distinctive slap, followed by a pitifully unconvincing "Ow," followed by a roomful of grins.

"The purpose of Meredith's and my endeavors," Jayne said, brown eyes flashing, "is to create new jobs for our local girls, so that they might have options other than becoming a rancher's wife right out of high school or moving to the city where there are better job prospects. Now, does anybody have a question for Meredith?"

"Are you married?"

"I mean concerning her store," Jayne insisted.

"You're living in the apartment over the store, aren't you?"

"What's your phone number?"

Jayne threw up her hands.

"Care to see a show with me?"

"How about dinner?"

The questions rang out from every corner of the room

with dizzying speed, making it difficult for Meredith to know which one to address first. The ad had said the bachelors of Jasper Gulch were shy but willing. An updated version would have to say they were more willing than shy. Still, they were delightful.

Before she'd opened her mouth to let them down easy, an old man whose thumbs were hooked in his suspenders exclaimed, "You boys can be a little more original than that. Why, you asked Jillian and Lisa those same dang questions at a meeting just like this one three years ago."

"I've got one," Ben Jacobs exclaimed as he scooted as far away from Mertyl Gentry as he could get. "Forget dating and marry me."

"A public marriage proposal has been done, too," Luke Carson said, tapping his palm with the gavel.

"You all remember what happened the night Wes Stryker went down on one knee and asked Louetta Graham to be his wife," old Doc Masey declared. "Wes didn't fare so well."

They all shook their heads forlornly, all except Wes and Louetta, who were now both happily married, only not to each other.

"Listen," Meredith said, holding up one hand. "I didn't come to Jasper Gulch in answer to your advertisement."

"You didn't?"

She shook her head. "I came here because this is where my niece and nephew are."

"But as long as you're here," somebody called.

She shook her head again.

"You mean you aren't planning to date?"

"Ever?"

She lifted one shoulder. "At least not for a while."

"How long's a while?"

Meredith hadn't planned to get into this tonight, but now

that the issue had been raised, she felt she should address it. "Well, not until I'm settled," she said, her smile genuine, her voice warm and sincere and just soft enough to be soothing. "To tell you the truth, I've promised myself one year free of making any sudden moves or rash decisions."

She found herself staring into a pair of moss-green eyes shaded by a brown Stetson. Sky's gaze was so direct and unsettling the pit of her stomach took a nosedive toward her toes.

Clearing her throat, she said, "I plan to make my home here, and I don't want to have any regrets." That said, she forced herself to look at the other people in the room. It seemed she'd scored some brownie points with the Ladies Aid Society, but not with the local men. Since the success of her business depended upon being liked, she hurried to say, "In the meantime, you're all welcome to stop by the store, to browse, and talk. I give great advice about patterns and color schemes and painting techniques, and my interior design rates are extremely affordable."

With a smile, she bid everyone goodbye. Keeping her eyes straight ahead, she strode to the back of the room through a crescendo of "aw shucks" and "rats" and "just our luck."

She glanced over her shoulder just before closing the door behind her. She could hear Luke Carson banging his gavel on the podium, but her gaze never made it that far. A lot of the men had crammed their hats back on their heads. She found herself staring into the eyes of the man who'd never taken his off. Her nerves fluttered. Lucky for her, the door closed before she got thoroughly lost in the depths of green eyes that were hooded by thoughts she couldn't begin to decipher.

* * *

"Somethin' wrong with that beer, sugar?"

Sky eyed his untouched bottle of beer, shaking his head at DoraLee Brown. "Just not thirsty, I guess."

Moseying on over to the Crazy Horse along with several of the other men had seemed like a good idea when the town meeting had adjourned an hour ago. Sky usually enjoyed talking and laughing and playing a game or two of cards. He'd told a joke he'd tried out on the hired hands at the Lone M that very afternoon. They'd laughed their heads off. Of course they had. It had the best dang punch line he'd heard in years. The Crazy Horse crowd had listened. And nothing. Nobody so much as cracked a grin. The only thing any of them seemed interested in doing tonight was talking about Meredith Warner.

"She wants to sell us paint and sofas and lamp shades," Neil Anderson said.

"Worse, she doesn't want to date anybody for a whole year," his brother, Norbert added.

"Why move to a town that advertised for women if you don't want to get to know the men?" Ben Jacobs asked, rubbing the spot where Mertyl had clipped him with two surprisingly strong arthritic fingers.

"To start a business, I guess," one of the other boys answered.

Sky pushed his beer a little farther away. He might as well leave.

"Who in Sam Hill would want to open a business here?"

Sky didn't quite make it to his feet. Droll or not, Norbert had a point. Why had Meredith decided to open her store here?

"Jasper Gulch ain't exactly a bustling metropolis."

That was true. Why open a store here and not in some

other small, but not-quite-so-dead town? Jasper Gulch suited Sky perfectly. But he wasn't trying to open a business.

Somebody dropped some quarters into the jukebox. Seconds later, a tune was being belt out about short skirts and men's shirts. Sky's mind wandered. As far as he was concerned, there was nothing sexier in the world than a woman wearing a man's shirt and nothing else. He'd seen Meredith that way once. She hadn't worn his shirt for long, because he hadn't been able to keep his hands off her. She'd reciprocated, touch for touch, coming to him so willingly, so womanly, so wantonly, he couldn't seem to forget it.

Something bothered the back of his mind. He was pretty sure he'd hurt her when it was all over, but he was nothing if not honest. So he'd told her the truth, and the truth was, he wasn't a forever kind of man. He'd been very clear about that. And yet she was back. Why? Sure, she wanted to be close to her niece and nephew. But she could have opened a business in Pierre, and commuted to work. Why was she really here?

He thought about the way her eyes had rested on him during that meeting. Twice. Both times she'd looked away before he'd figured out what it had meant. She hadn't looked at anybody else that way. He knew, because he hadn't taken his eyes off her.

Whoa.

What if she'd read more into those few hours they'd spent together than had actually been there? She was a woman, after all, and women tended to romanticize everything. What if she'd moved here because she'd convinced herself that passion was love, no matter what he'd said? What if she was saving her wiles to use on him? What if...

Sky dropped a few bills on the bar and rose blithely to his feet. He'd reached his truck when he noticed the lights on in the store across the street. Looking both ways, he strode on over, one last question, the most important question of all, running through his mind: What if he paid her a little visit and found out?

Pounding.

Meredith's eyelashes flickered, her eyes moving back and forth beneath her closed lids. The sound came again, a distant pounding, like a fist on wood. She must have been dreaming. Yes, that was it. She was dreaming, floating in a weightless, beautiful place filled with rainbows and the purl of wind chimes and a breeze more gentle and soft on her face than anything she'd ever felt. There were no doors in this place, so the pounding must have been coming from outside her dream.

Glass rattled. Meredith jerked in her sleep. She groaned softly and whispered, "So tired."

The rainbows dimmed slightly, but the wind chimes purled on and on. She floated close enough to the surface of her dream to realize that the other, disruptive sound had gone away. She sighed, snuggling deeper into the sofa cushions.

And then, suddenly, her eyes popped open. It took several blinks to bring the store into focus. She sat up groggily. She'd been unloading merchandise from boxes when exhaustion had overtaken her. She remembered leaning her head against the back of the sofa and closing her eyes for a moment. She glanced at her watch. Mercy, that had been an hour ago. She'd been sleeping so deeply she'd been dreaming.

Something must have awakened her.

She took a few steps toward the front of the store, peer-

ing at the door and then out the window. Other than a
handful of trucks parked in front of the Crazy Horse Saloon across the street, all was quiet out on Main Street.
Hugging her arms close to her body, she turned in a half-
circle, thinking that she might as well call it a night and
go upstairs to her apartment. She switched off one lamp.
Picking up the cordless phone she'd left on a low table,
she headed for the first open window.

A sound at the back of the store stopped her in her
tracks.

At first she thought it might have been the mother cat,
scratching at the door to go out. She glanced at the old
drawer Logan had padded for the stray and her seven kittens. The babies were sleeping; the mother stood, back
arched, poised for action, as if something had awakened
her, too.

The doorknob rattled. Somebody was trying to get in.

The blood drained out of Meredith's face, down her
neck, seeming to pool in the pit of her stomach. Pressing
her lips shut so no sound would escape, she forced herself
to settle down. She'd been robbed when she'd first moved
to Minneapolis. The thief had gotten everything, leaving
her penniless, destitute. She was almost thirty now. She
was older, wiser, and lately, too tired to start over again.
Everything she had was invested in this store, all her life
savings, her toil and sweat and dreams for the future were
tied up in the meager furnishings on this floor.

The doorknob jiggled again. Next, she heard a scrape,
as if someone was jimmying the lock. Panic rose in her
throat. There was no time to run upstairs. She wished she
had something to use as a weapon. She looked at the cordless phone in her hand. Wide awake now, she punched in
9-1-1, creeping stealthily toward the shadows in the back
of the room where she could hide.

The door burst open before she reached her destination. It was too dark to see who the intruder was, but she could make out the shape of a man. The cat sprang straight up, streaking between the intruder's legs. While the man was off balance, Meredith shoved an antique umbrella stand in his path. He tripped. "What the hell?"

She recognized that voice. As he fell toward her, out of the shadows and into the light, she recognized the face that went with it.

Sky's arms flailed, but he managed to keep from falling flat on his face. "Why did you do that?"

She backed up, straightening so fast she saw stars. "I'm trying to—" her voice seemed to be coming from far away "—defend my store." Sky's face blurred before her eyes, and all the world with it.

She swayed. Sky swore. He scaled a low table, catching her before she could hit the floor. "Easy," he whispered, but her eyes were closed, and she didn't hear.

He wrapped his arms around her, trying to hold her upright. It wasn't easy. He was the best roper in a hundred mile radius. He could rope a calf, hop off his horse, tie it up and hoist it onto his shoulder with ease. Meredith was slight, but right now, she was as limp as a rag doll, and a helluva lot harder to hold on to than a squirming, bawling, roped calf.

He swung her into his arms, staggering slightly. Keeping his feet squarely beneath them, he supported her head with his shoulder, then tried to decide what to do next.

Meredith's eyes fluttered. What happ...? Where am...? For the second time in a matter of minutes, she opened her eyes and tried to focus. This time, she found herself staring at the harsh lines of Sky's jaw. "What are you doing?"

"You're ill."

It sounded to Meredith like an accusation. She glanced

down, appalled to discover that she was in his arms. "Put me down."

"You fainted." Again, his voice sounded harsh.

"You scared me."

"Do you always faint when you're frightened?"

She never had before. She wiggled to get down, but his arms only tightened.

"I've been working hard, maybe too hard. I think I picked up a touch of the flu."

The flu in July? Sky couldn't think of a soul who had it this time of year. He couldn't think, period. Her scent was in his nostrils, her eyes dangerously close to his, her lips parted, her breath moist on his face. He wanted her to raise her face a little more, angle her chin slightly, so he could kiss her.

"Sky?"

"Hm?"

"What are you doing here?" she asked again.

Sky was trying to remember, really he was. It just wasn't easy to think. His adrenaline had kicked in, making him strong, and her weightless in his arms. It hadn't done a thing for his mental state.

"I saw the light on in the store, and I thought maybe we should talk. I knocked, but you didn't answer. My imagination conjured up several scenarios, and you were in trouble in every one. So I decided to try the back door."

"What did you want to talk about?" She'd spoken softly, her face inching closer.

Of everything he'd said, she'd picked up on that? "I didn't want you to get the wrong idea."

He loosened his hold, slowly lowering her feet to the floor. By the time she was standing, her entire body was indelibly imprinted on his. Both were breathing shallowly. Another second, another millimeter, and he would know if he'd been imagining the taste of her lips, the touch of her mouth, the passion of her kisses. Just a second, and a millimeter…

"Hold it right there!"

They jerked apart, and swung around. Sheriff Nick Colter burst into the room, one hand on his flashlight, the other on his gun.

"Nick!" Sky exclaimed. "For crying out loud, don't shoot. What are you doing here?"

Nick lowered his gun and his flashlight, but not his guard. He took a few steps closer, stopping between an antique trunk and a floor lamp. His gaze was assessing, his voice steady. "A 9-1-1 call came in from this number."

"You were fast!" Meredith exclaimed, still breathless.

"You called 9-1-1?" Sky asked.

She wet her dry lips, and pushed her hair out of her eyes. "I thought you were an intruder, or perhaps a thief."

"You two know each other?" the dark-haired sheriff of Jones County asked, watching them closely.

"No," Meredith said.

"Yes," Sky said at the same time.

She looked at Sky.

Sky looked at her.

They both shrugged.

"We've met," she said.

"Briefly," Sky amended. "But we don't really know one another, I guess."

Meredith averted her face because sometimes the truth hurt. "I fell asleep, and was awakened by a noise," she said to Sheriff Colter. "I thought somebody was trying to break in. It turned out to be a false alarm. I'm sorry, Sheriff."

Nick Colter and Sky were nearly the same height. They

both had dark hair and muscular bodies. The similarities stopped there. Nick had never been, nor would he ever be a cowboy. Until two years ago, he'd been a decorated police officer in Chicago. He'd come to Jasper Gulch because his then estranged wife and young daughter had moved here. He and Brittany had reconciled, and he'd stayed, taking over as sheriff of Jones County when Wyatt McCully had accepted a position on the police force in Pierre. Nick was more than qualified for the job. Meredith had a feeling his intuition was telling him more than either she or Sky had. He glanced around the store. "Looks like you're almost ready to open for business."

She could have kissed him for his tact. Instead, she walked with him toward the back door, which, until now, she hadn't realized was still wide open. "I'm planning to have a grand opening sale in a week or so. I hope you and your wife can join me."

"I'll tell Brittany." With a tug at the brim of his police hat, he left as quietly as he'd arrived.

Suddenly, the only sounds in the room were the resonant tones of the wind chimes high in the rafters. Meredith couldn't think of anything to say. Worse, she couldn't believe how close she'd come to kissing Sky. If Sheriff Colter hadn't arrived when he did, they could very well have been doing more than kissing right now. Whatever was between them was explosive. For a moment, when she'd discovered that she was in his arms, yearning had swelled inside her like it had that night a month ago. Now, something he'd said just before Sheriff Colter had interrupted them nagged at the back of her mind.

"What did you mean?" she asked. "When you said you don't want me to get the wrong idea. The wrong idea about what?"

She watched as he strode toward the door and scooped

his cowboy hat off the floor. His movements were fluid, graceful in a way that was uniquely masculine, uniquely Sky.

Worrying the brim of his Stetson with his callused fingers, he said, "I don't take women to bed often."

Something dangerously close to hope found its way inside her. A semblance of self-preservation kept her from letting it show.

"There's a good reason for that," he said. "Most women want a commitment, a relationship. And I can't offer either."

She glanced at his left hand.

"No. I'm not married. I intend to keep it that way. That's my point." His gaze was as direct as his next words. "You wouldn't be the first woman to see signs where there are only chicken scratches in the dirt. I meant what I said that night last month. I'm not the marrying kind. If you came back because I'm here, you're wasting your time."

Her back straightened and her chin came up a notch at a time. What an ego. Skyler Buchanan was a serious, smoldering man any woman in her right mind should avoid. He'd seemed so different that night over a month ago. For a few, brief hours, she'd believed she'd found a kindred spirit. She'd been wrong, of course, just like she'd been wrong about so many things in her life.

"Look," she said. "That night, I was reeling from the news that Kate and Dusty were forever lost to me. My defenses were down, my emotions were a mess, my heart was heavy. Don't worry. I'm not looking for a husband. Even if I were, I'd have to be an idiot to think you're husband material. Now, if you don't mind, I'd like to lock up."

Before Sky knew how it had happened, he found himself

staring at the peeling paint on the outside of her back door. He heard the lock turn. He was pretty sure the clunk that followed was a heavy piece of furniture being propped against the door. For some reason, that rankled.

She could take care of herself. That much was clear. Maybe he shouldn't have been so quick to put an end to what could have been another night of unforgettable passion.

Forget it, he told himself, cramming his hat on his head. Meredith Warner was putting down roots. No matter what she said, pretty soon she would want a man, a ring and a family. That made her off-limits to him. Now, if only someone would explain that to the part of him still reacting to the sight, scent and feel of her in his arms.

Meredith listened to the sound of Sky's retreating footsteps. Scrubbing a hand across her weary eyes, she turned very slowly, and finished closing the windows and turning out the lights.

She waited until she was in her apartment upstairs to commend herself for holding her head high, biting her tongue, swallowing her true feelings and keeping her pride intact. For a woman who was feeling under the weather, she'd handled that pretty well.

Her stomach pitched. Oh, she felt wretched. Lowering to the edge of her bed, she swallowed with difficulty.

Too exhausted to do more than swipe a warm washcloth across her face and brush her teeth, she slipped out of her shoes, peeled off her clothes, and slid between the sheets. Hopefully, whatever strain of flu she'd caught would be out of her system by morning.

Chapter Three

"Ohhh." Meredith closed her eyes and moaned softly, her hands braced on either side of the toilet rim. The only thing she'd gotten out of her system yesterday morning had been breakfast. It happened again today.

She wasn't well.

Cautiously testing the condition of her poor stomach, she rose to her feet in the little powder room near the front of her store. Evidently, South Dakota had more than the Badlands and winds that never ceased to blow. It had a strain of flu unlike anything she'd ever had before. It seemed to play hide-and-seek with her appetite and energy level. At times, she felt fine. She could be humming one second, and making a run for the bathroom the next.

She stared at her reflection in the antique mirror, then took a deep breath. Although she wasn't officially open for business, her first potential clients were due to arrive any second, and she so wanted to show them that she was quick-witted, knowledgeable and welcoming. She looked ghastly. Her skin was normally pale. Today, it was unnaturally so, her eyes red rimmed, her lips dry. She looked as if she'd been up all night, when in reality, she'd slept like a log for a solid nine hours two nights in a row. That was understandable. She'd been working hard. Why, she would have been worn out even without this unusual case of the flu. Her paint and wallpaper supplies had arrived yesterday. She'd unloaded boxes and boxes filled with gallons of paint, and cartons of wallpaper paste and wood stain, and cases of brushes and stencils and rollers.

Those sweet Anderson brothers had organized several of the other Jasper Gents to help her haul everything off the truck and into the store where she'd arranged the items on shelves. Sky hadn't been among them. She hadn't expected to see him. And she hadn't, unless she counted the moss-green eyes and legendary, one-of-a-kind swagger that had filtered through her dreams the past two nights.

She definitely wasn't well.

She splashed her face with cool water, then rinsed her mouth with mouthwash. She was dusting a little blush on her cheeks when the bell jingled over the door in the front of the store. Taking a calming, fortifying breath, she hurried from the powder room to greet her first clients.

"You would like your entire house redecorated?" Meredith asked the couple seated on the other side of the polished antique oak table.

"Not redecorated," Jake McKenna said matter-of-factly. "Decorated. It belonged to my father. It's no secret that he was a cold man. Maybe he cared about me in his own way, maybe he didn't. It's hard to say. If he did, he didn't show it. The house reflects his personality, and Josie and I want to turn it into not only a home, but our home."

Josie McKenna tucked a lock of long, wavy red hair behind her ear. "I'd like to do it myself, but..."

Jake covered his wife's small hand with his large, work-roughened fingers. "Josie's already added so much. Now that there's a baby on the way, there's just too much for her to do."

They looked at each other, seeming to get lost in each other's eyes. Reluctant to intrude on their moment, Meredith made a few notes on her sketch pad. Josie McKenna exuded warmth and friendliness. Jake, who owned the second largest spread in the entire area, was more reserved. He was a foot taller than his wife, and wore his hair a little too long to look civilized. On the surface, he appeared intense and intimidating. Anybody who took the time to look deeper saw a good, kind-hearted man completely besotted with his wife and her young daughter.

Meredith wondered how it would feel to be loved like that. The local bachelors had filled her in on the circumstances surrounding Jake and Josie's union. No matter what reasons they'd had for marrying last spring, they were deeply in love now.

"Jake's right," Josie said quietly. "It is a big house, and I don't want to overdo. But I'd really like to help."

"Of course," Meredith said, smiling. "You can be as involved as you'd like to be. Let's start by setting up a time when you can show me through the house, room by room. Then, you can tell me what you envision, what you'd like, what you don't want, that sort of thing."

"How about this afternoon?" Josie asked.

The redhead's enthusiasm was contagious. With her pen poised over her notepad, Meredith grinned. "I'd love to drive out this afternoon, but I promised Wes and Jayne that I'd watch Logan and Olivia." Not that Meredith bought that story. But if Jayne wanted to pretend that Meredith didn't believe with her whole heart that Jayne was simply helping Meredith form a loving bond with the children, who was she to argue?

"Bring them along," Josie insisted. "Kelsey loves to play with other children."

Meredith considered it for a few seconds before nodding. "I'll clear it with Jayne and Wes. If it's okay with them, we'll be there this afternoon. I'll need directions."

Jake took over. "The Lone M is fifteen miles southwest of town."

The Lone M?

Meredith hoped no one heard her sharp breath. Although she jotted down names of roads and landmarks, it was only for the sake of appearance. She'd spent part of a night there in the bunkhouse where Sky lived.

Oh, she knew the way.

Two nights ago, he'd made his views regarding relationships crystal clear. Even if his touch had indicated that he was fighting a strong attraction to her, his words, his expression, even his stance had let her know exactly where he stood. No matter how much he wanted her physically, he wasn't planning a repeat performance. Evidently, to him, that was all it had been: The first act in a one-curtain play. She was the only one who had to know how much it had meant to her.

According to the Jasper Gents, Sky Buchanan was Jake's right-hand man. It stood to reason that if she worked with Josie to redecorate the main house at the Lone M, her path would cross Sky's. He wouldn't like that.

Meredith flattened her hands on the table's smooth surface. Whether sparks flew between her and Sky or not, she needed this project. She needed the work, the money, the sense of purpose and accomplishment it would bring.

Seeing Jake and Josie McKenna to the door, she decided

that all she could do was stand back as far as possible, where those sparks couldn't reach her.

Five minutes into her visit to the Lone M, Meredith had relaxed. She needn't have worried about running into Sky. Jake had introduced her to two young ranch hands when she'd first arrived, but she'd been lucky. She hadn't seen so much as a glimpse of Sky. It was the middle of the afternoon, and he was probably out on the range. It was turning out to be her lucky day.

Her luck held throughout the tour of the McKenna house. What a place. They started in the kitchen. By the time they'd gone through the entire house, Meredith was giddy with excitement. Josie had already done a lot toward making it homey, but there was so much more Meredith wanted to do. The open staircase could use a new runner, the stone fireplace a colorful screen. All the heavy draperies would go, new fabrics, patterns, colors added to every room. Jake liked leather; Josie preferred floral prints. Meredith planned to incorporate both tastes in the decorating scheme. Her mind whirled at the possibilities.

"Well?" Jake said from the front porch when the tour had ended. "When can you start?"

Meredith laughed out loud. "I'll begin putting together ideas and working up some sketches as soon as I get back to the store."

Jake kissed his wife and shook Meredith's hand before sauntering down the porch steps and on out to a large shed beyond the corral. Meredith said goodbye to Josie, then called, "Olivia, Logan. Time to go."

The kids appeared from around the corner just as the telephone began to ring inside. Josie excused herself to answer it, and the two little girls sashayed to Meredith's side and each reached for her hand. "Come see my new filly," Kelsey exclaimed. "My new daddy says I can ride her when we're both bigger."

Meredith glanced toward the barn. The coast was clear. There was no sign of Sky. Apparently, her luck was still holding. "All right. Show me your new pony."

"It's not a pony." There was exasperation in Logan's voice. "A pony is a small, full-grown horse. A filly is a baby horse. A pony is always going to be a pony, but a filly is only a filly until she's four."

Exasperated or not, her ten-year-old nephew was as smart as a whip. His father had been a rodeo champion, so it stood to reason that Logan would have a vast knowledge of horses. But it was more than that. The boy seemed to have an innate connection to the large creatures. He ran up ahead, climbing the fence and perching at the top. A big black horse came over to him immediately, a baby at her side. The mother horse nuzzled his neck, trying to get into his pockets. Logan's giggle brought a smile to Meredith's face.

He's happy, she thought. Despite tragically losing his parents, and then having to move to a new town, start over in a new school, with everything he'd been through, he was happy.

He jumped down the moment the girls arrived at the fence, and promptly dug several sugar cubes out of the front pocket of his faded jeans. "Here," he told the little girls. "Remember. Keep your hands flat and your fingers together."

The girls nodded solemnly, and did as he instructed. They were adorable—Kelsey with her red hair fluttering down the back of her yellow shirt, and Olivia, whose hair was dark like her mother's had been, her little hand held out so trustingly.

"Let your Aunt Meredith try."

Even if Meredith hadn't recognized Sky's voice, the way her heart fluttered would have made the glance she cast over her shoulder unnecessary. Sky stood just outside the shade of the barn, twenty feet away. Particles of dust and hay glittered, floating on a slanted ray of sunshine behind him.

"Go ahead," he said.

She wasn't thrilled at the idea of placing her hand anywhere near that big creature's teeth. That, however, wasn't the cause of her sudden case of nerves. She considered admitting that she was afraid of horses, but those animals were an integral part of Logan's life. He loved them, and she loved him. Taking a deep breath, she accepted the sugar cube, and followed Olivia and Kelsey's lead.

To her amazement, the horse was gentle, her soft muzzle tickled Meredith's palm. She laughed. It felt good, almost as good as the answering grin on Logan's face.

"Uncle Sky!" Kelsey exclaimed, vying for his attention the second he sauntered closer.

"Hey, Red." He settled the child in one arm as if it was the most natural thing in the world.

"When are you gonna let me ride Bommer?" Logan asked.

"When your Uncle Wes says you're ready, I reckon."

"Rats," Logan answered.

As long as Meredith didn't allow herself to look at Sky, she could pretend that she wasn't aware of his every move.

"Meredith's gonna help Mama fix up the house," Kelsey told Sky.

"That so?"

Meredith felt his gaze. "Well, kids" she said. "We should…"

"Let's play a game," Olivia interrupted. "Come on Kelsey, Logan." The child was bright.

"Olivia, I don't think…"

"Hide-and-seek." Logan was no dummy, either. Spinning around, he said, "'Livia, you're it. Come on, Kelsey, let's hide."

Sky lowered Kelsey to the ground. Just like that, the kids ran off to play in the side yard. Without them to act as a buffer, the bottom drained out of Meredith's stomach like sand in an hourglass.

In the background, she could hear Olivia as she began counting into a tree. "One, two, three, four, ten, eleven, nineteen, twentyteen."

Meredith shook her head. "They're very good at that."

"They're urchins."

Surprised, she peered up at him.

He shrugged. "All three of those kids have survivor instincts. They're going to be okay."

There was something about his straight nose, strong chin, and the squint lines beside his eyes that made her think it takes one to know one. He hitched one boot onto the lowest board, absently stroking the horse's neck. "What do you think of Jasper Gulch so far?"

It was an innocent question. Therefore, it couldn't have been the question that confused her.

In the distance, Olivia was still counting. "Twenty-five, twenty-six, thirty-one…"

"It's very quiet."

He seemed to be waiting for her to continue. When she didn't, he said, "That's it? It's very quiet?"

The man was far too appealing for her peace of mind. He'd hurt her. And she wasn't going to encourage him or give him an opportunity to do it again. It would have been nice if her brain had alerted her lips, because she grinned despite her resolve not to.

She gave the entire area a sweeping glance. Flowers

bloomed in bursts of colors near the wraparound porch and throughout the yard. An old-fashioned swing hung from the branch of a hundred-year-old tree.

"Forty-seven," Olivia said. "Fifty. Ready or not, here I come."

"It's true," she said. "Sounds carry differently out here."

Right then, the sound of Logan's voice would have carried to her ears no matter where he was. "You didn't count to fifty. That's cheating."

"I did so, and it is not."

Meredith and Sky exchanged a similar look. The kids argued on and on. "Sounds do carry differently out here," Meredith said. "Even voices. Maybe it's because there are no squealing tires, hissing brakes, or honking horns to drown out the natural sounds, no tall buildings to obstruct them."

She'd wondered if she might miss the city. Strangely, she didn't. It was peaceful here. Every day felt more promising than the last.

A herd of cattle lumbered across the pasture in the distance, an occasional moo carrying on the breeze. On the other side of the fence, horses neighed, the filly, which wasn't a pony at all, whinnied.

"Kids!" Meredith called.

They ignored her, of course.

"Do they do this often?" Sky asked.

"What? Argue? Oh, yes."

Sky adjusted the tilt of his hat against the angle of the sun. "One of these days they'll realize that there's enough room for both of them, in the world, in this town, and in their own family."

She stared at his profile. "You were an only child, weren't you?"

She'd expected him to smile. When he didn't, she looked more closely. Something passed through his eyes, like the shadow of pain, or regret, a secretive glimmer that flickered for a moment before disappearing. It gave her pause. She had a feeling Skyler Buchanan hadn't always been a footloose and fancy-free spirit. She'd sensed it the first time they'd met. So, she thought, she hadn't been wrong about everything that night.

"You hafta go back to the tree and count again!" Logan insisted.

"Do not."

"Do so."

Kelsey, the smaller of the two girls watched as if in rapt fascination. Olivia didn't let Logan's size intimidate her. Meredith could tell he didn't like that, but he didn't cross the line between verbal and physical battle. Finally realizing she couldn't win this one, Olivia stomped off toward the tree. Logan could have gloated, but he didn't.

"Logan and Olivia are at that age when everything feels like a contest," Meredith said. A light came on in her head. "That's it!"

"What's it?" Sky asked.

"I haven't been able to choose a name for my store. And I've just found a solution. I'll make it a contest."

"You're open for business and don't even have a name? Isn't that a little like putting the cart before the horse?"

She tried not to bristle, but it wasn't easy, because she tended to jump into situations with both feet when she should have been testing the water with her big toe. "I'm not technically open for business." Her mind raced ahead. She would give the people of Jasper Gulch the opportunity to submit potential names for the store. And then she would choose her favorite.

Voila! She'd been searching for a name for her store,

as well as a way to entice people to come in and shop.
Now she had both.

"Hear that?" Sky asked.

The kids were no longer arguing. It was icing on the
cake.

"Hey, kids!" Sky called. "Keep the silence down a
little, would you?"

Kelsey giggled from her crouch behind the lilac bush.

"The kids like you," Meredith said. Directly in front of
her, the big horse's eyes fluttered in rapture beneath the
gentle stroke of Sky's hand. "The horses seem to, too."

"Why wouldn't they?"

This time, she held his gaze. "No reason."

"You don't sound very convincing."

That had been her intention. Still, she fought valiantly
not to give in to the impulse to smile.

"What's the matter?" he asked. "You don't think I'm
a likable guy?"

"You can be very charming when you choose to be."

He hitched one boot on the lowest board and inched
slightly closer. "I'll be more careful in the future."

He wouldn't be. In his way, he was charming her right
now.

They shared a smile. When his gaze dropped to her
mouth, they shared something else, something dangerously
close to desire. Skyler Buchanan was rugged and lean and
more than a little brash. She wondered what he kept hidden
behind his cocky smile and cowboy swagger. Oh, there
was something. She'd sensed it the first time they'd met.
Now she was sure.

"What?"

She didn't bother apologizing for staring. "I think
there's more to you than what you want people to see."

Sky didn't know what to say to that. He wasn't accustomed to talking to women who were so straightforward. Since Meredith had turned her head, he took advantage of the opportunity to study her profile. Her long, straight, shimmery hair was fastened on the back of her head, exposing the delicate curve of her ear, the smooth skin at her temple, the shadow beneath her cheekbone. At five foot seven, she was taller than a lot of the women out here. She reminded him of a willow switch, slender, yet strong enough to bend without breaking.

Something smelled good, and it wasn't the horses or the hay. He remembered that scent. He was reacting to it in the most basic way. "I am exactly what you see, Meredith."

She turned her head, staring into his eyes for a long time. "If you say so."

Oh, no, she didn't. He wasn't going to be put off that easily. "I'm a semi-nice man who doesn't clean up too bad. I like nothing more than the wind in my face and the world at my feet."

"A semi-nice man. Yes, I believe that is what you are."

The way she said it made him feel understood. That could be a dangerous thing. And yet, with her, it didn't feel dangerous at all. She knew where they stood. He'd been wrong about her. She wasn't like other women who spouted superficial compliments about his green eyes, or his lanky build, or the way he looked walking away, in order to win his favor. Maybe he shouldn't have ended things after that one night.

"Why are you smiling?" she asked.

He hadn't realized he was. "Oh, I was just thinking that I haven't exactly been hospitable since you arrived in town. As long as you know where I stand, you're welcome to stop by sometime. Anytime."

She eyed him for a full five seconds, her eyebrows lifting in identical arches. "Maybe I will," she said.

He eased a little closer.

She held her ground and lowered her voice. "When every other man falls off the face of the planet."

Sky chalked one up to the visiting team. "That could take a long time."

"It would most likely take forever."

He grimaced. "Forever isn't my favorite word."

"I'll alert the press."

"I'd appreciate it."

Neither of them smiled, and yet Sky found himself thinking that they could have been friends, if it wasn't for this unholy attraction between them that seemed to take on a life of its own. Yearning coiled inside him. Easy, he told himself. Time to hit the road, or the dusty trail. Time to get out of here before he found himself wishing for things that just plain and simply couldn't be.

"Remember," he said, giving the brim of his dusty, brown Stetson a tug. "The invitation stands."

He took a backward step, scaled the gate and disappeared inside the shadowy interior of the barn.

"Do you kids think it's hot in this car?" Meredith turned her face into the wind rushing in her window.

In the passenger seat, Olivia clutched her stuffed goose, hugging it close, her eyes drifting shut tiredly.

"Yeah," Logan said from the back seat. "Uncle Wes says it's hotter than a witch's whistle, just the way he likes it."

"Do you like the heat?" she asked, feeling a stab of remorse because she didn't know.

"I like fall the best."

"So do I," Meredith said.

When he grinned, she did, too. Day by day, a bond was forming between her and Logan and Olivia. She still missed Kate, and she wasn't sure she would ever forgive herself for waiting too long to try to reconcile with her only sister, but for today, she felt all right. The idea for the contest, the chance to be part of Logan and Olivia's lives, not just from the sidelines, but in an active role, was all coming together. She believed it took a village to raise a child. And Meredith was becoming a part of that village. A welcome part.

Even her relationship with Sky had improved. Perhaps relationship was too strong a word. If they'd met under different circumstances, they probably could have been friends. If she hadn't put the cart before the horse, like he'd said. If she hadn't jumped in with both feet before testing the water.

But she had, and there was no turning back.

She rounded a corner, pulling onto Old Stump Road. It was dusty and riddled with so many chatterbumps she was getting nauseous. She slowed down to a crawl. Without the wind streaming through her window, sweat broke out on her forehead. Her throat convulsed.

Oh, no. She recognized the sensation.

Pulling to a stop, she threw the lever into park and staggered out of the car.

"What's wrong?" Logan asked.

"I'll be right back."

She made it to the ditch in the nick of time.

When she turned around, she saw that Logan and Olivia had gotten out of the car, too. Olivia eyed her strangely. Finally, the little girl said, "Kelsey's mama does that, too."

"She does?" Meredith's voice sounded far away in her

own ears. The hand she scrubbed across her face felt surprisingly clammy. Maybe she should see a doctor.

Olivia nodded sagely. "Her mama throws up every morning."

Meredith's stomach roiled. Easy, she told herself, testing her legs to see if they were operational again. Trying to concentrate on something else, she whispered, "Every morning?"

Again, Olivia nodded sagely. "On account'a she's gonna have a baby."

Logan's head whipped around. He studied Meredith in that thoughtful, assessing way that always reminded her of Kate. "Are you gonna have a baby, Aunt Meredith?" he asked.

"What?"

"He said, are you gonna have a baby?" Of all times for Olivia to come to her brother's aid.

A baby?

The idea was so ludicrous Meredith almost laughed. She wanted to laugh. She tried to laugh. Suddenly, laughter was beyond her.

In order to have a baby, she would have to be pregnant. And in order to be pregnant, she would have had to...

A Chinese gong went off inside her skull. The times she'd felt ill, and dog-tired, and faint. She wet her lips, working hard to combat the nerves that clamored in the pit of her poor stomach. "I think I have the flu, kids."

"Oh." The girl was obviously disappointed.

Logan didn't comment, but he continued to watch her closely.

"I'm pretty sure I have the flu," Meredith said, louder than before.

"That's good, Aunt Meredith," Logan said. "Because you're not married."

"Yes," Meredith answered, climbing dazedly back into the car. "I know."

Chapter Four

Meredith's haze of confusion continued into the evening and late into the night. It had even filtered into her dreams. She was normally a morning person, but today she woke up feeling groggy, sluggish. Pushing her hair out of her face, she trudged to the bathroom where she'd placed the home pregnancy kit she'd picked up in Pierre last night. The procedure was relatively straightforward and took only a matter of minutes. She was staring at the little wand that came with the kit when her haze lifted.

She wanted it back.

Positive. It was positive. According to the kit, she was pregnant.

It couldn't be accurate. There had to be some mistake. She read the directions again. She'd followed them to the letter. Maybe the kit was faulty. Whatever happened to the good old days depicted in old black-and-white movies when results such as these required an old doctor with wire-rim glasses saying something to the effect that the rabbit had died? These little kits were probably good for the rabbits.

Meredith absolutely could not believe it when she smiled. At least her sense of humor hadn't deserted her.

Her stomach roiled. She bent over the toilet as she had the previous two mornings. This wasn't funny. When she was finished, she splashed her face with cool water, picked up the little indicator wand and stared at the positive symbol.

It wasn't an optical illusion. She'd checked the calendar, and had done a little mental math. She'd been so busy moving and getting her store ready to open that she hadn't noticed that she was slightly more than two weeks late. She couldn't blame that on a faulty kit. Then there was the nausea and the fatigue. Separately, they could have indicated that she had the flu. Put them together and it added up to a lot more than that.

She was pregnant.

Her thoughts whirled as if short-circuited. This time, she hadn't jumped in with both feet. She'd fallen through a hole in the vortex of reality, landing in a world that looked exactly like the old one but felt nothing like it. In this new world she felt as if she'd been run over by a truck.

She hadn't been run over by a truck. She was pregnant. She was pregnant. She was pregnant. Oh, good Lord, she was pregnant.

She could count on one hand the men she'd been with in her entire life. Actually, she would only need three fingers. If she went back four years, she would only need one.

One man was all it took.

She knew that, of course. But they'd taken precautions. She also knew that aside from complete abstinence, few precautions were one hundred percent foolproof.

An image of a tiny baby wrapped in a soft blanket shimmered across her mind. A baby. Both hands spread wide over the flat of her stomach covered by the oversized T-shirt she slept in. Beneath her hands, cells were multiplying, and a tiny human being was already growing. She wondered what the child would look like. Would her baby have blond hair and brown eyes like her?

Or would this child have green eyes? Like Sky.

Oh, my God. Sky.

Her own reflection swam before her eyes. Sinking to the edge of the bathtub, she bent over, putting her head between her knees. When her lightheadedness passed, she lifted her head and swallowed the tightness in her throat.

What had she done?

She'd come to Jasper Gulch because Logan and Olivia were here. She was getting to know them, and they were coming to love her. All she'd wanted to do was carve out a niche so she could live a quiet life in a quiet town near them.

What was she going to do?

Slowly, she stood. There was so much to take in, she could hardly think. Hugging her arms close to her body, she strode out to her bedroom. She was too new in Jasper Gulch to have made the kind of friends she could turn to at a time like this. Oh, Jayne and Wes had been wonderful, but she didn't know them well enough to know how they would react to a woman in her situation. Her parents had both died years ago. Not that she could have gone to them even if they had been alive. Her mother had gotten pregnant at seventeen. Meredith's father had married her. As far as Meredith could tell, the only thing he'd contributed to the union had been another baby two years later. He'd cleared out shortly after she'd been born. It hadn't taken Meredith or Kate long to pass their mother when it came

to emotional maturity. They'd both survived, but childhood hadn't been golden.

Meredith had tried Boston, up-state New York, then
worked her way West to a little town twenty miles west
of Chicago. She'd spent one summer in Nashville, and one
harrowing winter in the Colorado Rockies before settling
in Minneapolis. But she hadn't gone anywhere near Texas
where she and Kate had grown up.

Suddenly, Meredith wished Kate were here. Sadness
washed over her as it did so often when she thought of
her sister. Kate had left home when Meredith had been
fifteen. She remembered it all so clearly, the tears, the
disbelief, the feeling of being abandoned. Looking back,
she realized that was the real reason she hadn't contacted
Kate all those years. Oh, if only she could go back, she
would do so many things differently. For one thing, she
wouldn't blame Kate for getting out, for saving herself.
Kate had been too young and too poor to save Meredith,
as well. That had been up to Meredith to do. As soon as
she could, she'd done it, too. Oh, she'd stumbled along
the way, but she'd always picked herself up. She'd learned
from her mistakes, and she'd never made the same one
twice.

This was the first time she'd ever found herself pregnant, that was for sure. A smile came out of nowhere,
stealing across her face. It baffled Meredith almost as
much as the knowledge that she was going to have a baby.

She had a lot of difficult decisions to make, but that one
had been made for her. Now, she had to get her feet back
underneath her, and figure out what to do next.

"You're in excellent health," Dr. Kincaid said.

Meredith tucked a strand of hair back into the bun on
the back of her head and murmured an appropriate re-

sponse. In his late thirties, Burke Kincaid wore a white dress shirt, dark pants and a blue tie. His medical diploma had come from the state of Washington. He'd moved to Jasper Gulch a year or so ago to take over old Doc Masey's practice. Meredith had liked him the instant he'd walked into the little examination room and introduced himself before beginning.

When she was dressed again, Dr. Kincaid had returned. Rather than sitting behind an imposing desk, he'd pulled up a stool and wheeled it a few feet away from her chair. It put them on the same level, and made him approachable. She'd considered finding a doctor in Pierre where no one would know her. She was glad she'd chosen this doctor whose office was located in the front portion of an old house on Custer Street, his family's living quarters in the back and upstairs.

She was, indeed, pregnant. The little home pregnancy test she'd taken three days ago had been right on. She'd made several important decisions since then. Her feet were firmly underneath her once again.

"I'd say you're approximately five weeks along," Dr. Kincaid said levelly.

Although she made no comment, there was nothing approximate about this. She knew precisely when this child had been conceived.

"You're a little on the thin side," Dr. Kincaid said. With a smile, he added, "But pregnancy usually remedies that." He'd already prescribed vitamins, told her to eat plenty of fruit and vegetables and protein, and to avoid spicy and greasy food. He'd assured her that morning sickness was normal. Her body was simply adjusting to this new condition.

"Normally," he said, "nausea subsides after a month or two. In the meantime, I want you to eat right, get plenty of rest, and avoid stress. Later on we can discuss birthing options, labor coaches, et cetera. Will the father be an active participant?''

Meredith didn't know how to answer. Sky had been an active participant five weeks ago. Bravely holding the doctor's gaze, she said, ''He doesn't know.''

Dr. Kincaid nodded solemnly. ''Would he want to know?''

She thought about the way Sky was with Kelsey McKenna and Logan and Olivia. Would he want to have an active role in his own child's life? ''I don't know, doctor,'' she answered truthfully.

He nodded, but made no further inquiries, and offered no advice. ''Unless you have more questions, I believe that's all for today,'' he said. ''I'd like to see you in a month. Crystal will schedule the appointment.''

They both stood. ''Thank you, doctor. There's one more thing. I would appreciate it if news of this didn't get out just yet.''

His smile was genuine as he said, ''If Jasper Gulch gets wind of it, it won't be from this office.''

He walked her to the reception area, then disappeared into another examination room. Crystal Galloway looked up from the front desk. ''There,'' the other blonde said with a wink. ''That wasn't so bad, was it?''

Meredith pulled a face, and Crystal chuckled, bringing Meredith's smile out of hiding. A little older than Meredith, the receptionist exuded femininity. They were nearly the same height, but Crystal had an American accent Meredith couldn't place. Her eyes had an exotic slant and were the palest green Meredith had ever seen. There was something mysterious about Crystal Galloway. Everyone in town said so.

"If you want to talk," Crystal said, "or catch a movie, or even rent a video, I'm free most nights."

Her warmth and sincerity was touching. "Thanks," Meredith said. "I'd like that."

By the time she left the office, she knew she was in good hands. She still didn't know what to do about the situation with Sky, but the rest of her life seemed to be taking shape. Jayne had loved her idea for hosting a contest to name her store. A flyer already hung in the front window. Word was all over town. Several of the area bachelors had already stopped in to buy paint and to make suggestions. Neil Anderson thought she should call it Peach Tree Corners, after the scent of her shampoo. Mertyl Gentry had poked her head in two days ago. Petting her gigantic cat with arthritic fingers, she'd suggested calling the store Calico Corners. Someone else had suggested Tabby's Antiques. All of them were good suggestions, but not quite what Meredith had in mind, not that she knew what she had in mind. Gathering up fabric swatches and paint samples to show Jake and Josie McKenna, Meredith only knew she'd recognize it when she heard it. The grand opening extravaganza was slated for two weeks from today. She would reveal her choice then.

Two hours later, Meredith was heading back toward town. Josie and Jake had narrowed down their choices for the upholstery for the sofa and armchairs, but couldn't decide about the curtains. All in all, they were making great progress. Jake had handed her a check to cover preliminary expenses. She'd told him it wasn't necessary, but he'd insisted it was the right thing to do.

His words played through her mind during the drive back toward town. The right thing to do. The right thing to do.

She'd seen the doctor, her business was nearly up and running, but she hadn't told Sky she was pregnant. In only three days, she'd gone from complete shock to absolute awe at the prospect of becoming a mother. She wanted this child. It was that simple. And that complex. Having a child out of wedlock didn't have the negative social ramifications it once did in the rest of the country, but what about here? She could endure people's censure. The thought of her child enduring it made her ache. She wasn't ashamed, far from it. What was best for her baby? Did this child deserve to know its father? And did Sky have the right to know?

Suddenly, she knew that telling him was the right thing to do. Slowing down, she checked for traffic, then did a U-turn in the middle of the dusty country road.

Sky ran the currycomb down the filly's sleek side. "Atta girl."

He gave the horse a thorough brushing, keeping the bunkhouse door in plain view all the while. He and the boys had been moving the herd to greener pastures when he'd seen Meredith's car in the distance. Buck and Billy had noticed her conservative sedan, too, and had started talking about the contest she was hosting and how the winner would get an entire room decorated for free. Both men had agreed that they could think of a better prize. Sky had seen red, or perhaps it was green. Either way, he'd made sure he was back in the barn before she left, just in case she'd changed her mind and took him up on his standing invitation to return.

He'd kept the front door of his bunkhouse in plain view. Therefore, he knew for a fact that she hadn't wandered on over to chat, or anything else.

If she was trying to make him humble, it was working.

The trouble was, he didn't think she was trying to do anything. This wasn't a game to her. She had too much class for that. He'd known it the first time he'd laid eyes on her. Something had passed between their gazes that night. Need had built, exploding around them like fireworks on the Fourth of July. It had been a long time since he'd felt such a reaction to a simple look. Shoot, he was reacting to the memory of it right now.

Buck and Billy had headed into town. A few minutes later, Sky saw Meredith's car pull out of the driveway. He decided to call it a day.

Ten minutes later, he was wishing he'd gone into the Crazy Horse with Buck and Billy. He'd leafed through his junk mail, looked inside the refrigerator three times and the cupboard twice. In no mood to open a can of stew or hash, he headed for the shower.

He stood beneath the spray for a long time, letting the water pummel his head and shoulders, shampoo and soap suds flowing down his body to the drain. His thoughts strayed to Meredith all over again. Shoot. He turned the temperature down slightly. He wasn't a fan of cold showers, but they had their uses. With a flick of his wrist, he cranked up the cold water. And cringed.

This was crazy. The day hadn't been great all the way around, and it was going downhill fast. He was thirty years old. He should have been old enough to control his own lust. All right, he thought, turning the water off. He was a little disappointed, but it wasn't anything a good, hard run on Bommer wouldn't relieve.

Reaching for a big towel, he dried his face and hair. The rest was hit and miss. He wrapped the towel around his waist, then left the bathroom in search of clean clothes. A movement out of the corner of his eye stopped him in his tracks. Meredith was standing on his front stoop, the back of her blond head visible through the window. Heading for the door, he eased into a smile. His day had just gotten a whole lot better.

Meredith looked out over the land stretching as far as the eye could see. Her first knock on Sky's door had gone unanswered. She'd waited a few minutes, and tried again. It, too, hadn't been answered. Evidently, Sky wasn't home.

She strode to the railing, and was on the first step when hinges creaked behind her, drawing her around. Sky stood in the doorway wearing a towel, a grin, and nothing else.

She averted her eyes. "I came at a bad time."

"You're timing's perfect. Come in."

Nerves clamored in her stomach. Instead of making her nauseous, they left her unnaturally warm. Or maybe that was Sky's doing. "I thought no one was home."

"I was in the shower."

Yes, she could see that.

"Come in."

She must have moved, because the next thing she noticed, Sky had closed the door and was gesturing her farther into the room. "It's been a long day. I'm glad you stopped by."

She wondered if he would still say that when she finished saying what she'd come here to say. Searching her mind for a way to begin, she glanced around the sparse room. In days gone by, the building had been used as a bunkhouse. Now, this room held an old sofa that had seen better days, a television, and a lot of clutter. "I love what you've done with the place."

He sauntered closer, seemingly completely unembarrassed that he was practically naked. The man had far too much nerve for her peace of mind. He moved with an easy grace, a kind of loose-jointedness one automatically associated with a cowboy. He had thick, black hair, the shadow of a heavy five o'clock beard, and yet his chest hair was sparse. His shoulders were wide, his arms muscular, his stomach ridged like a washboard. Again, she averted her eyes, then moved purposefully to the other side of the room.

"I haven't done anything with the place, Meredith. It's decorated in early squalor, just like it was the last time you saw it. If I remember correctly, neither of us was concerned with the décor. You remember that night, don't you?"

His voice was a low murmur, a gentle sweep across her already oversensitized senses. She swallowed, nodded. "That's why I'm here."

"If it's any consolation, I haven't been able to forget that night, either. Seeing you around town isn't helping."

"It isn't?" Was she mindless?

He shook his head and eased slightly closer. "On the surface, you're pretty, and slender, and strong. But I know what's underneath. I know how sultry your sighs are, and how responsive the smooth skin on the side of your neck is to my lips, how supple your thighs are, and the ticklish places on the insides of your knees. Every facet of your passion is like hidden treasure. A man could go crazy with desire while he's discovering what's beneath the next layer, and the next. But what a way to go."

Meredith's mouth went dry, her thoughts turned hazy. She was mindless, all right. She'd come here to talk to him, to tell him…

"A man would have to be a fool not to try. I'm a lot of things, but I'm no fool."

She was lulled by the deep, husky tones of his voice, lured by the slow burn in his eyes. She hadn't been close to many men in her life, and she'd never been close to a man like Sky. He made no attempt to hide the fact that he was watching her. He made even less of an attempt to hide the fact that he liked what he saw. He wanted her. Just being in the same room with him sent anticipation and a heady sense of urgency racing through her. It lowered her eyelids, and her defenses.

He reached a hand to her face, taking the touch he needed. Her gentle sway toward him seemed to be all the encouragement he needed. His arms wound around her back, and his lips touched hers. The same thing had happened that night last month, that night...

She'd responded to him the first time she'd seen him in the little diner on the highway just outside of Pierre. Now, she felt an even greater tug on her emotions. It was more than desire, more than lust. She'd been lonely for a long time. But what she felt in his arms wasn't simply a remedy to loneliness, either. She'd been sad that first night. She wasn't nearly as sad anymore, and yet whatever she'd felt then was even stronger now.

He moved his lips across hers, drawing a moan from deep in her throat. Her lips parted, softening, the kiss deepening. In a matter of seconds, it became a kiss full of need, full of giving, and taking. Her thoughts swirled together, making her forget why she'd come, making her forget everything except this moment with this man.

"I've been dreaming of this." The kiss must have broken, because he was talking, his voice low, suggestive, his fingers deft, gentle, sure.

When she opened her eyes, she discovered that she and Sky were in his bedroom. His towel was holding on by a thread. He whisked her shirt from her shoulders, down her arms. And then his hands covered her breasts, the thin fabric of her bra all that was between his flesh, and hers. She strained into his touch, his groan matching her own.

Her bra came off next, and then his hands found what they'd been seeking. "Hidden treasure," he whispered moments before his lips followed the course his hands had taken.

Meredith's head tipped back, her eyes closed, and yearning found its way to the very center of her. She heard the scrape of a drawer, and then he came back to her, a glimmer of what was to come deep in his eyes.

"I wouldn't want history to repeat itself," he said, his voice a husky murmur. They were almost to the bed when he kissed her cheek, her chin, the little hollow below her ear. "I'll keep you safe. Don't worry, I'll make sure the gene pool stops with me."

Her eyes opened. "The gene pool?"

"Other than you, I haven't been with a woman in years. You don't have to worry about that. And you sure as hell don't have to worry about me getting you pregnant."

He had no idea how right he was about that. Meredith's heart pounded an erratic rhythm. She cleared her throat. "Would that be the end of the world?"

"Trust me. The world doesn't need another Buchanan. But I need this. Don't you?" He touched her again, intimately, reverently almost. "So beautiful, so lush, so many hidden treasures."

His touch was heaven, but she couldn't pretend she hadn't heard what he'd said. "Sky."

He must have felt her stiffen, for he placed a gentling hand to her hair. It reminded her of the way he'd caressed the horse a few days ago. Meredith wanted nothing more than to push her disquieting thoughts aside, and to give in to the need between them. But she had someone else to consider.

"Sky, we have to stop."

"Honey, we haven't even gotten started."

"I mean it." Trying for a lighter tone and a small smile, she added, "I didn't come here to do this."

Although she spun around, she felt his eyes on her. Spying her shirt draped over a chair, she grabbed it and put it on.

"You have no idea how sorry I am to hear that."

She glanced at him. There was no reproach in his eyes, but there was warmth, and a seductive glimmer that reminded her of the way he'd looked that night last month. That night their, no, her, child had been conceived.

She buttoned her shirt with shaking fingers. "I have to go."

"So soon?"

His stab at humor was the last thing she'd expected. She wondered if he had any idea what it did to her. His bedroom was small. He stood between her and the doorway. In the tight space so near him, she couldn't think of a single thing to do or say. She was so shaken she didn't notice the towel slip from his body until it was almost too late to avert her gaze.

She had to get out of there. If only her fingers would cooperate. The moment she managed to fasten the last button, she rushed past him, straight out of the bunkhouse, and climbed behind the steering wheel of her car.

She was at the end of the long driveway when she realized her shirt wasn't buttoned right. She would fix it later, when she was miles away. Glancing down, she saw that she'd forgotten her bra. Not about to go back for it now, she pulled onto the road and headed for town.

Sky heard the door open, heard a car start. Since he couldn't very well rush after Meredith buck naked, he pulled on a pair of jeans. It wasn't easy. His legs weren't fully operational, and his brain was even less so. By the time he'd raised the zipper and followed her outside, her car had disappeared in a cloud of dust.

He stared at the road until the dust had cleared. The shuddering breath he took smelled like deep summer and felt like deep frustration. The first night she'd visited him had turned out a lot better. Scrubbing a hand over his beard-roughened jaw, he went back inside, slamming the door behind him.

Meredith's visit had wiped out whatever good the cold shower had done him. After donning a shirt, any shirt, he dug up a pair of socks. He was in the process of putting them on when a scrap of white caught his eye. Leaning down, he snagged the delicate strap of a satiny bra with one finger. He glanced toward the door, toward his bed, then toward the wastebasket next to his dresser. Swearing under his breath, he hung the undergarment on a peg near the door, shoved his feet into his boots, and crammed his dusty hat onto his head. Without waiting for his breathing to return to normal and the blood to return to his brain, he rushed into the barn. It was what he should have done in the first place.

"For a minute there," he said to his favorite horse, "I thought today was my lucky day. For crying out loud, I thought my dreams were coming true."

Bommer tossed his head and snorted.

Sky heaved the saddle onto the big animal's broad back, then paused, staring at the view. Beyond the wide barn doors, McKenna land stretched as far as the eye could see. Some men dreamed of owning land. Not Sky. He didn't have many dreams. Lately, the ones he did have had been invaded by a willowy blonde.

"She claimed she didn't come over to make love," Sky said, tightening the cinch. "What other reason could she have had for stopping over?"

The horse stared into Sky's eyes. Sky sighed. "You're probably wondering how I can expect a horse to understand women when man can't. What do you say we go for a hard run?"

Bommer strained toward the door the instant Sky swung into the saddle. Moments later, man and horse were rushing headlong through the evening twilight, racing the wind, and outrunning the question nagging the back of Sky's mind.

If Meredith hadn't come to make love, what in Sam Hill had she been doing there?

"Aunt Meredith?"

Meredith opened her eyes and glanced at the little girl standing in the doorway. "What, sweetie?" Meredith had only been lying down for a matter of minutes, hoping it would be enough to rejuvenate her before the grand opening began.

"Are you gonna die?"

"What?" Meredith sat up gingerly. She was learning that if she moved slowly, and nibbled on saltines, her nausea generally subsided. "Why would you think that?"

"Logan said."

Meredith glanced at the clock on the bedside table, and then at Olivia, who looked adorable in her sleeveless red dress and white sandals. Everything was ready downstairs. Balloons bobbed in the breeze, wind chimes purled. Everything in her store was polished and in place.

Nearly two weeks had passed since her disastrous visit to Sky's house. She'd half feared he would show up out of the blue and demand to know what she'd been doing at his place that day. The idea alone mortified her. She needn't have worried. She hadn't seen him since that night. He'd drifted into her thoughts more often than she would have liked, but she hadn't had much time to sit around feeling sorry for herself.

The McKenna project was progressing nicely. Also, the rest of the new furniture had arrived and was now arranged in the store. Paint and wallpaper supplies were selling well. She'd already placed an order for more. The contest was officially over, and the new sign was up. Thanks to the artistic talent of Dr. Kincaid's wife, Louetta, it was truly beautiful.

Meredith had taken Dr. Kincaid's advice. She ate right, and rested every day after lunch. She'd seen the kids often, and had taken them to a movie in Pierre three days ago. Now that she thought about it, Logan had watched her closely all the while. The poor boy. He'd already lost both his parents, and now he was worried about her.

Reaching for Olivia's hand, Meredith strode out to the living room where Logan had been watching a video. He stood up the instant she entered the room.

"We have a few minutes," she said. "Let's all sit down."

"I knew it." Logan spun around so quickly his shiny new cowboy boots scudded on the floor and the ends of his bolo tie got crossed. "You're sick, aren't you?"

"I'm not sick, Logan."

"The flu doesn't last weeks and weeks."

Beneath his defiance, she knew there was real fear. She lowered to the sofa, smoothing her loose fitting skirt over her knees. "That's true. I don't have the flu."

"Then what's wrong with you?"

She looked at the children. Five-year-old Olivia hovered near her big brother, her bedraggled stuffed goose clutched beneath her arm, her eyes as big and blue and round as his.

"Well," Meredith said. "I have some good news. Some

happy news. I'd planned to wait a little while to tell you. Can you two keep a secret?''

"I can. I'm not so sure about 'Livia."

"I can, too."

Meredith rushed in before an argument broke out. "I'm not sick, kids."

"You're not?"

She shook her head.

"Then why do you p—"

She cut Logan off, saying, "I'm going to have a baby." She smiled because this was the first time she'd said it out loud.

"No kidding?" Logan quipped.

"No kidding."

"So that's why you're sick all the time?"

She nodded wryly. "It's called morning sickness, and it's getting better. Now, I didn't really plan to have a baby just now, but I'm very happy about it. I love being your aunt, and now I'm going to be a mother, too."

"I thought you had to be married to have a baby," Logan said.

Meredith tried not to take longer than necessary to consider her answer. After all, one wrong move could bring on a barrage of questions. She wasn't prepared to answer questions regarding the birds and the bees, and yet she wanted to put their minds at ease. "It's nice if parents are married when they have a baby. I truly believe that. Sometimes, though, it doesn't work that way. Sometimes, there are different kinds of families."

"You mean the way me'n Logan and Uncle Wes and Aunt Jayne and you are all a family?"

Meredith beamed at her niece. She couldn't have said it better herself.

Logan turned serious eyes on her. "Are you gonna get married?"

"I don't think so, sweetie."

"Are you gonna leave?" Olivia asked.

"I don't want to." The thought of leaving Logan and Olivia, her only family, made her ache. "You and Logan are here. And the store is here. This is where I want to be. But I still have decisions to make, and until I make them, I'd like you to keep this a secret."

The kids nodded gravely, and Logan asked, "Are you gonna get fat?"

Meredith chuckled. Patting her flat stomach, she said, "At least right here, I am."

"I guess that'll be cool," Logan said.

Meredith's heart brimmed with love. And she did something she hadn't done, but had wanted to do for a long time. She hugged the kids, and pressed a kiss along each of their smooth foreheads. Something magic happened. They hugged her back.

The bell jingled downstairs, signaling their first customer. Logan and Olivia spun around and were already halfway down the stairs by the time Meredith had swiped her fingers over the moisture on her cheeks, and followed.

Logan and Olivia were coming to love her, and accept her. Meredith hoped that in time, the townsfolk would accept her, too.

The bell jangled again. Goodness, the place was filling up fast. The murmur of voices carried to Meredith's ears as she descended the stairs. Some, she recognized; others were new.

"Guess what, Aunt Jaynie?"

Meredith smiled at the lilt of excitement in Olivia's

tone. Mercy, that child had a voice that could penetrate steel.

"What dumpling?"

"Aunt Meredith's gonna have a baby."

Chapter Five

Meredith stood, frozen on the last step. For once, she didn't feel faint. She felt stricken. There were at least two dozen people in her store. She'd heard Olivia's proclamation. Had everyone else?

She could stand people's censure, but she didn't want her child to have to endure it. She wasn't ashamed, and she wasn't going to hide her pregnancy once she started to show. She'd thought she would have a few months to decide how to handle people's speculation, what to say, how to explain. Olivia hadn't given her much time.

Logan was glaring at Olivia, who was peering up at Meredith, looking as dumbfounded as Meredith felt. All three of the Anderson brothers, and a few other cowboys she'd met only briefly, had formed a circle around the punch table. Jayne was the only adult paying any attention to Meredith. Maybe she was the only one who'd heard. Please, Meredith said to herself, let that be the case.

The bell over the door jangled again as Jake, Josie and little Kelsey McKenna joined the grand opening celebration. A sudden gust of warm July air streamed through the open door, setting the chimes high in the rafters jingling. Olivia ran over to Kelsey. Moments later, the two little girls were on their way to the back of the store to see the kittens. By the time Jake and Josie had accepted the punch Crystal Galloway was ladling near the front of the store, Meredith had recovered slightly.

Descending the last step, she pulled a face at Jayne, who was waiting for her at the bottom, her dark eyebrows raised above sky-blue eyes. "Never trust a five-year-old to keep a secret, any secret."

"Do you think anyone else heard?" Meredith whispered.

"Then it's true?"

When Meredith nodded, Jayne flipped her red feather boa over her shoulder with a dramatic toss and mouthed, "Congratulations. You can tell me all about it later." With a wink, she set off across the room.

Meredith had never met a woman who could dress so eccentrically and still look so put together. Watching her go, it occurred to Meredith that Jayne hadn't answered her question. Still, she felt better. A lot of it had to do with Jayne's immediate acceptance and complete lack of criticism.

"Afternoon, Mer'dith." Neil Anderson stepped into Meredith's path, his hat in his hand, his gaze everywhere except on her. "Er, that is, nice party."

"Thanks, Neil. Have you had some punch and cookies?"

"Yes. Um, that is, yes."

She and Neil had become friends these past few weeks. In his mid-thirties, he was slight of build and wiry. Meredith's quick glance around the room caught half the men off guard. They rallied quickly, averting their gazes.

The word was out.

Resigning herself for whatever was to come, she asked, "What can I do for you, Neil?"

He blushed, his Adam's apple bobbing slightly.

"Relax," she said, smiling and meaning it. "It isn't contagious."

He met her eyes suddenly, and in their gray depths, she saw something honorable and touching. He glanced at her left hand and quietly asked, "Are you married?"

She raised her chin a notch, and shook her head only once.

"Engaged?" he asked.

Again, she shook her head. "I'm as single as a long-stemmed rose."

"That's good." He paused, and shrugged sheepishly. "At least it's good for the Jasper Gents."

Meredith's grin grew in direct proportion to the earnestness in Neil's expression. "Thank you, Neil, but I'm not so sure everyone in town is going to agree with you."

"Donchoo worry about the fine folks of Jasper Gulch. These small-town people might have big opinions, but they have big hearts, too. Give folks a chance to get used to it, and they'll come around." Leaving her with that dose of advice, Neil moseyed on over to talk to his brothers.

It didn't take long for word to spread throughout the store. By the time the grand opening had begun to wind down, Meredith had been the object of a lot of speculation, but strangely, Neil was right. For the most part, the people in Jasper Gulch were amazingly kind. Meredith was more convinced than ever that Jasper Gulch was exactly where she wanted to live, and work, and raise her child.

By four o'clock, the punch and cookies were nearly gone, and her head was practically spinning. She'd sold eight gallons of paint and one sofa. What's more, she'd had three requests for dates and two marriage proposals. What she really yearned for was a nap.

"It's time for the grand finale!" Jayne declared, capturing everyone's attention. "Let's move this party outside, shall we?"

The twenty or so remaining guests meandered out to the sidewalk. By the time Meredith had gathered the basket she'd prepared for this event and joined them, everyone was talking about the new sign she'd had installed high on the front of the store.

"Just look at that artwork!" Forest Wilkie declared.

"And to think," Butch Brunner added, "that until last winter, nobody knew our very own Louetta Graham had such a talent."

"That's Louetta Kincaid, now," Dr. Burke Kincaid, her new husband declared.

Meredith heard what everyone was saying, but for some reason, she found herself following the movement of every vehicle that drove by. She thought she caught a glimpse of Sky's silver pickup truck round the corner down the street. Before she could be sure, a middle-aged rancher in a ten-gallon hat vied for her attention and blocked her view. The next time she glanced at the street, the silver truck had disappeared. Meredith told herself she wasn't disappointed.

"Are you gonna keep us in suspense all day?" Butch asked.

Peering at the crowd, she asked, "Suspense?"

"Yeah. You gonna give us a name, or do you want us to guess?"

"A name?" Meredith's throat went dry.

Jayne breezed to the front of the crowd and quietly said, "I believe Ben's referring to the name of the individual who won the contest, Meredith."

Oh. Of course. They only wanted to know who had won the contest. Flushing slightly, Meredith smiled at the people closest to her. "First of all, I want to thank those of you who made suggestions. It wasn't an easy choice. After much deliberation, I narrowed it down to four. Tabby's Antiques would have been perfect if it were only an antique store, and Peach Tree Corners would have been lovely had the store been located on the corner. I liked Kate's Cellar, too, in honor of Logan and Olivia's mother, my sister." She gestured to the beautifully painted vines twirling across the letters Louetta Kincaid had fashioned out of antique chests, lamps and floral arrangements. "But this one seemed perfect."

She handed out gift certificates for paint, mood candles, and decorative wreaths to the three runners-up. Consolation prize in hand, Melody Carson said, "Who's the lucky person who came up with the name you chose?"

"Yeah, who's the winner?"

Meredith was in the process of stammering through a reply when a deep voice called from the back of the crowd. "I guess that would be me."

Everybody turned around, craning their necks for a glimpse of who'd spoken.

"Who said that?"

"Can you see?"

"I cain't see a thing."

Meredith's heart thudded; she knew that voice by heart.

The crowd parted, and there was Sky, feet planted a comfortable distance apart, his hands on his hips, his head tilted slightly, his eyes in the shadow of the brim of his brown Stetson. He took a deliberate step in her direction. "I guess you could say it came straight from the horse's mouth." He ambled closer, moving with that easy grace folks automatically associated with cowboys of old. "Isn't that right, Meredith?"

Her face felt stiff, her smile pasted on, but she nodded.

"You entered the contest, Buchanan?" Neil Anderson asked.

Sky answered without taking his eyes off Meredith. "Not exactly."

"Then I don't understand how you..."

Meredith cleared her throat of the nerves that had taken up residence there. "Sky didn't officially enter the contest, but he's the one who gave me the idea to name my store Hidden Treasures. I added the remainder of the name, Antiques and Fine Furnishings."

"Then it looks like he's gonna get the prize," one of the bachelors said forlornly.

"Some people have all the luck," another of the Jasper Gents said, giving Sky's back a half-hearted slap.

Sky nodded, but he had yet to break eye contact with Meredith. Eyeing the two of them shrewdly, Jayne clapped her hands and exclaimed, "I'd say that's a wrap! Party's over, folks. Thanks for coming everyone."

"Yes." Meredith forced a brightness she didn't feel. "Thank you all for making Hidden Treasures grand opening a success. Please stop in anytime. I'll be happy to answer any questions you might have about decorating or painting. I have a lot of experience in interior design, and I'll help in any way I can."

One by one, the guests said their goodbyes. Some of them climbed into the assorted vehicles parked at the curb. Others wandered on across the street to the Crazy Horse Saloon. Leaving Jayne to say goodbye to Sky, Meredith returned to the store, where she began tossing used napkins and plastic cups into a wastebasket, and tried to get her breathing to return to normal.

She'd discarded all the paper products and had gathered all but the last two helium-filled balloons when the bell over the door jingled behind her. "Jayne, do you think Logan and Olivia would like these balloons?"

Silence.

"I used to love balloons when I was small. My friends kept them in their rooms until the helium seeped out. Not me. I always took them outside and set them free, watching them drift higher and higher until they disappeared." She grew quiet for a moment, remembering. She hadn't thought of that in a long time.

"Memories are funny, aren't they?" she asked. "That particular one reminded me that my childhood wasn't all bad."

Her revelation was met with more silence.

"Jayne?"

"I sent Jayne home, Meredith."

There was that voice again. Meredith turned slowly. Taking a deep breath, she stared at Sky. His eyes had darkened with an unreadable expression. Seven weeks ago, he'd changed her plans for the evening with one heart stopping smile. He wasn't smiling now. She had a feeling that somewhere in the dark recesses of his mind he knew exactly what he was doing. It would be nice if he would let her in on the secret.

"Look." She gestured to the store with a sweep of one hand. "It's been a long day. So, if you don't mind..."

"That's just it," he said, slowly striding closer. "I do mind."

Meredith's heart pounded an erratic rhythm. Sky made no attempt to hide the fact that he was watching her. She cleared her throat, pretending not to be affected, and reminded herself that he'd made his position regarding commitment and relationships crystal clear. She didn't owe him anything, except maybe her gratitude for his part in creating the baby growing within her. It was amazing how much she already loved this child. She didn't know why Sky had come here, but she doubted it was to hear the truth. *She* wanted this baby. She didn't want a man who didn't feel the same way.

Sighing, she said, "The store is officially closed for the day, Sky. If you'll excuse me." Forbidding her legs to shake, she continued on toward the back of the store and deftly untied two more balloons.

Sky recognized a hint when someone hit him over the head with it. He chose not to take it. Following Meredith to the back of her store, he wished she didn't move quite so effortlessly, wished his eyes weren't so drawn to the way her pale blue skirt swished with every sway of her hips, wished his body wasn't reacting to the sight of her this very minute. Everything about her was quiet, understated. She'd been a quiet lover, too, not given to noisy cries or sudden outbursts. The sounds she'd made had been more like soft sighs and deep, sultry whispers.

Just being in the same room with her sent anticipation and a heady sense of urgency racing through him. Normally, it took a midnight run on Bommer to quell it. There was nothing normal about this.

They were in the back of the store where he'd jimmied the lock a few weeks ago, where he'd caught her when she'd fainted. Now he knew why she'd fainted.

"You're pregnant." He couldn't help it if it sounded like an accusation.

"You heard."

That was it? That was all she had to say? "The seasons might drag out here, Meredith, but news travels faster than the speed of light."

"I've noticed."

Sky thought men were supposed to be the "yup" and "nope" talkers. Women had the reputation for talking up a storm. The problem was, Meredith wasn't like other women. Consequently, he wasn't sure what she was going to do next.

She untied the last balloon, her hair falling to the front of her right shoulder, the ends resting along the upper swell of her breast, which appeared fuller than he remembered. Sky cleared his throat. "Well?" he asked.

She glanced up at him, "Well, what?" written all over her face. At least he had her attention.

"Are you going to tell me who the father is?"

Her jaw dropped slightly. Finally, a reaction.

"I hope you're not planning to try to pin it on me."

Her fingers went slack, and the balloons floated, unheeded, up to the rafters. "Pin it on you?"

"I admit that I was unpardonably reckless that night, but I wasn't careless."

She stared at him far longer than he considered polite, then said, "You want a name?"

Sky decided to overlook her snide tone. He hadn't been expecting an actual name. All he'd wanted was an exoneration of sorts. He started to answer, but she cut him off.

"Or would you prefer the entire list? Let's see. I could give it to you front to back, back to front, or in alphabetical order. How far back did you want me to go? Five years? Ten, fifteen?"

He was so intent upon studying the way her eyes flashed with indignation that he didn't realize she'd backed him into the alley until he felt the breeze on the back of his neck. She held his gaze, she wet her lips, and in that quiet way she had, she said, "Why not make it easy? In the past four years, I've been with only one man." While the implication was still soaking in, she moved backward. "But don't worry. I wouldn't marry you if you were the last man on earth.''

The door slammed. And Sky blinked. The new lock clicked into place.

He took a backward step, turned to his right, and then to his left. For crying out loud, the woman had him going in circles, and she wasn't even trying.

Was she telling him the truth? God, how did a man know for sure? He couldn't. Sky should know. He'd been lied to most of his life.

He ran a hand over the stubble on his chin, on up his face and across his eyes. An hour ago, he'd been minding his own business, picking up a few groceries at the J.P. Grocery store. He hadn't been paying much attention to the clucking hens of the Ladies Aid Society until one of them mentioned that Meredith was in the family way. An unwelcome tension had settled in his stomach. He'd had no intention of confronting her, but he'd seen the group of people in front of her store, and a force greater than him had taken control of his legs. The next thing he knew, he'd ambled on over. He still wasn't sure why he'd opened his mouth, taking credit for the name she'd chosen for her store. After all, when he'd murmured the words 'hidden treasures,' he'd been referring to the plump softness of her breasts, the sound of her sighs, the scent of her skin. She hadn't disputed his claim. Which just went to show that she was probably lying about the number of men she'd been with, too.

A movement out of the corner of his eye caught his attention. Tipping his head back, he watched as a red balloon strained free of a high branch, then slowly floated out of sight.

He swept his hat off his head, raked his fingers through his hair. What in the hell had she meant, she wouldn't marry him if he were the last man on earth? Cramming his hat back on his head, he stomped on around to Main Street where he'd parked his truck.

Who'd said anything about marriage?

Meredith's clock radio burst on for the third time. She couldn't hit the snooze again. She had to get up. She wanted to bury her head beneath her pillows and go back to sleep for an hour. Or three or four. But she had to get up. There was work to do, a store to open promptly at nine. She dragged herself out of bed. Munching on saltines and sipping cool tap water, she prepared to begin her day.

At five minutes before nine, she pulled her apartment door closed behind her. She was halfway down the steps when a splotch of bright blue caught her eye. She peered at the balloon hovering at the ceiling, its colorful string swaying on the invisible current of air high in the rafters. From her vantage point, she counted eight others. She remembered untying the strings, but until now, she'd forgotten all about those balloons. She must have let them go during Sky's visit late yesterday afternoon.

She continued on down the steps, thinking that those balloons would come down to earth when the helium seeped out. Heaven knew she had.

Sky didn't believe this baby was his. She hadn't been prepared to defend her character, at least not to him. The fact that he believed she was promiscuous hurt. She hadn't known what to say to try to change his mind. Late last night, she'd decided not to try. Surely all this negativity would have an adverse affect on the baby. She needed a positive attitude and outlook, and vowed that from now on, she would have both. From now on, she would think pleasant thoughts and make constructive plans for her future.

A knock rattled the glass in the front window. She paused only long enough to take a deep breath. Grasping the doorknob more tightly than was necessary, she turned the lock and opened the door to the last person in the world she'd expected to see today.

Sky walked in and promptly removed his hat. She stared wordlessly at him, and he at her.

"May I help you?" she finally asked.

His hair was black, his eyes a mossy shade of green, his jaw set. When he finally answered, his voice was quieter than she'd expected. "Now there's a question."

Meredith had no idea how to reply to that. The lower portion of his face was darkened by a two- or three-day beard, his eyes red rimmed, as if he hadn't slept well. He held up a hand. "Don't say it. I know I look like something the cat dragged in."

Her guard slipped a notch. She felt a curious, swooping pull at her insides. "No matter how bleary-eyed and tired you look, Sky, you're still not as bad as the unsightly little creatures Peaches the cat drags in."

"Thanks. I think."

Meredith's guard slipped another notch. It occurred to her that she liked him. The sentiment left her amazed and shaken. She told herself it was only natural to feel this way. He was, after all, the father of her unborn child. Wasn't it normal for a pregnant woman to be more emotional than usual? In keeping with her earlier vow to maintain a positive attitude and a sunny outlook, she wavered him a smile and said, "I'm sorry about yesterday, Sky."

"You are?"

She nodded earnestly. "I've had a few weeks to become accustomed to the idea of a baby. It's only understandable that it came as a shock to you yesterday."

Sky studied her unhurriedly. The sunlight slanting

through the front window washed her in a golden haze, surrounding her like a halo. It was an optical illusion, for Sky knew firsthand that women weren't angels.

"When is, that is, when do you think…" He cleared his throat and tried again. "What I'm trying to say is, when does the doctor say…"

"Are you asking when the baby is due?"

Her voice was soft and deep, and full of a compassion he didn't want and sure as hell didn't need. "Yeah. I guess that is what I'm asking."

"In early February."

Sky swallowed. He'd done the mental math. February was the month he'd come up with, too, on the off chance that their one night together had produced a baby. Not that he believed it had. He raked his fingers through his hair and began to pace.

"What's on your mind, Sky?"

Her voice drew him around. She was wearing a long skirt and sleeveless shirt in a subtle, subdued shade of gray that matched the shadows under her eyes. She looked pale, delicate, almost ethereal and beautiful in a way she hadn't been before. Sky imposed an iron will on himself. This was no time to turn to mush. Drawing himself up to his full height, he said, "You wouldn't be the first woman to claim a child was one man's, when it was actually another's."

Meredith had known he was going to say something serious before he'd said it. She didn't know him well, but she was coming to recognize the subtle nuances and changes in his expressions. She felt on the verge of understanding something important about him. Choosing her words carefully, she asked, "Has that happened to you?"

"Not to me," he answered.

"But it's happened to somebody close to you."

He didn't reply one way or the other. Oh, he wasn't ready to believe he was the father of her child, but he couldn't seem to discount the possibility, either. Before her stood an honorable man who was grappling with his conscience. She hadn't been wrong about him that night nearly two months ago, at least not completely. On a fundamental level, he was a good, decent man.

"Know what I think?" she asked.

"Are you asking if I know what goes on in the deepest recesses of a woman's mind? I don't have a clue."

His expression was severe. She smiled anyway. "I think that if we'd met under different circumstances, we would have been friends."

Sky took a quick sharp breath, then snapped his mouth shut. A kick in the knees would have been easier on him than the woman-soft smile Meredith wavered at him. Yearning washed over him. It was all he could do to tamp it down deep inside him where it had been for as long as he could remember.

He stared wordlessly at her. No matter what she claimed, he wasn't sure he could believe her. He had damn good reasons for steering clear of her. There was no excuse for the need running through him, no excuse to want to reach a hand to her face, and take the touch he needed.

He raised his right hand toward her, but the bell over the door jangled just then, drawing her attention, and she didn't see. Neil Anderson ambled in just as Sky lowered his hand to his side.

"Neil, hello!" She strode toward the front of the store, stopping halfway between the two men. The next time she looked at Sky, her face still wore the smile she'd given Neil. It rankled.

"Hey, Sky," Neil called.

Walking closer, Sky didn't reply.

Looking from one to the other, Neil said, "You stop by to talk to Meredith about your prize, Sky?"

"Prize?" Sky asked.

"Prize?" Meredith said at the same time.

Neil cast them an uncertain look. "You did win the contest."

"Yes, he did," Meredith said. "Win the contest, that is." Turning to Sky, she said, "You'll have to let me know which room you want redecorated, and when you would like me to begin."

With a nod at Neil, Sky started for the door.

Meredith murmured something to Neil, then fell into step beside Sky. "Don't worry," she whispered for his ears alone. "Your secret is safe with me."

Sky made it out of the store while his legs were still operational. He'd been right about one thing. A kick in the knees would have been a lot easier to handle than kindness doled out in the form of a smile and a woman's whispered promise.

Jake McKenna shoved his chair away from the table in the center of Mel's Diner and rose to his feet. "You in a hurry to get back to the ranch, Sky?"

Fork poised over the slice of homemade cherry pie he hadn't touched yet, Sky shrugged. "I don't have anything to do at the Lone M that won't keep."

Jake dug a five-dollar bill out of his pocket and dropped it on the table. "I'll be back in about half an hour."

Sky nodded. Chances were, Jake was going to do something as ordinary as get a haircut or go to the post office. At six foot two, he was long in stride and short on explanations. Sky never asked for any. In return, Jake asked few questions of Sky. Theirs was a friendship based on quietude and trust. The ground rules had been established the day Sky had shown up on the Lone M needing work and a roof over his head the summer he'd turned seventeen. Although the ranch belonged to Jake, the two of them worked the land side by side. Once, Jake had offered Sky a piece of it. Sky had declined. He came and went as he pleased. Owning land would only tie him down.

Digging into his pie, Sky didn't pay much attention to the conversation going on all around him. The town's only diner wasn't big, but it was clean and the food was decent. Every day had its own special. Mesquite steak on Monday, meat loaf on Tuesday, rib eye and baby potatoes on Wednesday, scalloped potatoes with baked ham on alternating Thursdays, and three-siren chili on Friday. A person could get a cheeseburger, fried chicken or a sandwich any day of the week, and liver and onions the first Tuesday of every month. It was predictable. Sky liked that about it. There were ten tables, eight booths, and a hat rack by the door that pretty much went unused. The faded awning outside matched the checkered curtains at the windows. Nobody cared. Folks came to the diner for food and gossip. Without fail, they went away with plenty of both.

Sky was thoroughly enjoying his pie, so there was no reason on God's green earth why he glanced up simply because the old hinges on the door creaked when someone opened it. Once his gaze fell upon Meredith, her arms laden with fabric swatches and wallpaper books, he couldn't look away.

Although she said hello to a few of the local boys, she didn't so much as glance in Sky's direction. As was typical for the diner crowd, talk turned to Meredith the instant she disappeared into the kitchen.

"She don't look in the family way to me," old Roy Everts said to his brother, Hal.

"The wife says it's early yet," Hal answered. "What do you suppose she's doing in the kitchen with Louetta?"

"I hear tell Louetta's thinking about fixin' the place up a little. And she's gonna pay the Warner gal to help her."

"According to Norma Zammeron, the Warner gal's been keeping mighty busy these past two weeks," somebody else said.

"She was busy weeks before she came to Jasper Gulch," Clive Hendricks said, his voice dripping with sarcasm and innuendo. "If you know what I mean."

The pie in Sky's mouth tasted sour. He knew what Clive meant. Everyone did. He supposed it stood to reason that at least one of the local men would view Meredith in a bad light. After all, she was a pregnant woman who had no intention of getting married. No one came out and said she was easy, but the old double standard was alive and well in this neck of the woods, at least as far as Clive Hendricks was concerned.

Lowering his fork to the table, Sky left his pie unfinished. No matter what he'd insinuated to Meredith two weeks ago, he didn't believe she was anything less than he'd been: A person who, for one brief night, had been raw with need. That didn't mean he believed he was the only man who'd brought out those needs in her.

He'd seen her from a distance several times in the past two weeks, but he'd only come face-to-face with her once since that morning in her store when she'd told him his secret was safe with her. She'd looked him in the eye, then quietly averted her gaze. There was no excuse for the need running through him, no excuse for wanting her again.

It would help if he could forget how she'd felt in his arms. Maybe that would have been easier to do if it hadn't taken place in his bed. More than likely, he was fooling himself. Making love to her would have been unforgettable no matter where it had happened.

Standing, Sky dug a five dollar bill out of his pocket and left it on the table next to Jake's.

"I can't tempt you with a refill?" the pretty young waitress asked, holding a coffee carafe in each hand.

"No thanks, Brandy."

"You can tempt me any time you want," Clive said.

"It doesn't take much to tempt you, Clive," Brandy said with a grudging smile.

"Can I help it if I'm all man? Hey, Brandy, how much longer is the Warner woman gonna hide in the kitchen?"

"Meredith isn't in the kitchen. She dropped off some fabric samples and wallpaper books then left by way of the back door."

"That's too bad. Now there's a woman I wouldn't mind getting closer to. Why buy the cow if you can get the milk for free?"

If Sky could have turned around at the door without causing a scene, he would have marched over to Clive's table and told him what he could do with his snide comments and outdated pearls of wisdom. God knew Sky had caused more than one stir these past few weeks. He'd ridden Bommer at breakneck speed, and driven his truck the same way. On those occasions when he went into town, he'd kept his ears and eyes open, watching, listening, waiting for Meredith to 'claim' to somebody in town that he was the father of her baby.

The rumor hadn't surfaced.

She'd kept her word. In the back of his mind, questions hovered. What if she was telling the truth? What if the baby was his?

His stomach knotted as if he'd taken a fist in his midsection. If the baby was his, the Buchanan gene pool that had been dredged from the bottom of the bog and consisted of sludge and slime wouldn't stop with him.

If the baby was his...

He adjusted his hat against the high noon sun and peered across the street. Clayt and Melody Carson and their two little boys were on their way out of the grocery store. Clayt had the older child on his back. The toddler strained to get out of Melody's arms. That kid was a spitfire with a cherub smile and downy hair. Although one of the boys looked like Melody and the other like Clayt, there was no doubt they were both Clayt Carson's boys. They acted just like him.

Sky wondered how it would feel to be so sure of something like that. Was Meredith telling him the truth? What if she was? What if the baby was his? The question was driving him crazy.

He happened to glance down the street just as Jake stopped talking to the old-timers shooting the breeze underneath the barber pole, and strolled inside. It looked as if Sky had some time to kill.

There was something he had to do.

It took only a matter of seconds to walk to the curb and reach through the open window of his truck, retrieve the paper bag he'd stuck in his glove compartment, then cut through the narrow right-of-way between the diner and the J.P. Clothing store. In the back alley, his steps slowed, his boots crunching on loose gravel. The sweet scent of honeysuckle hung heavy on the warm air. Other than the twitter of birds and the buzz of a lone honeybee, it was quiet in the back alley. A scrawny mother cat was stretched out on her side, feeding a whole slew of kittens in the patch of sunshine spilling through the open door. Being careful not to disturb them, he walked inside.

It took a moment or two for his eyes to adjust to the

dim interior. When he could see again, he found Meredith looking up at him. She was on her knees, scissors in one hand, pins in the other.

He scooped his hat off his head. "I've been thinking."

"You have?" She moved to get up.

He halted her with a lift of one hand. "This won't take long."

Settling back on her heels, she said, "Yes, Sky?"

She was looking up at him, her eyes big and brown and so deep a man could lose himself if he wasn't careful. "People are talking."

"People?"

"Some people. About you. And I've been thinking, about what you said. About the baby being mine."

"Yes?" she asked quietly.

Gripping his hat so tight the brim would never be the same, he said, "Mostly, I've been thinking about what I should do, you know, just in case."

Chapter Six

Meredith's gaze made a slow sweep from Sky's eyes to the death grip he had on his Stetson. He'd entered the store silently. Looking at him now, she understood why people said it was the quiet ones you had to watch. She'd overheard two local women complaining that their menfolk would sleep in their hats if they could get away with it. Sky was different. He took his hat off when he was in the presence of a woman. If the timing were right, she would ask him where he'd acquired his manners. But first things first.

"You don't have to do anything, Sky. I've let you off the hook, remember?"

He shook his head as if unsatisfied with her answer, and thrust a crumpled paper bag into her hands. "I know you said you wouldn't marry me if I were the last man on earth, but I think you should reconsider, just in case."

Just in case?

No matter what he'd indicated, this wasn't something she could talk about on her knees. Leaving the pins and scissors on the sofa cushion she was reupholstering, she stood up. "Just in case the baby's yours?"

He had the decency to flinch. "I didn't mean that the way it sounded."

Meredith had a feeling he'd meant it exactly the way it had sounded. Again, she felt on the verge of understanding something important about him. Giving him the benefit of the doubt, she said, "Marriage is a big step, Sky."

"You think I don't know that?"

He glanced beyond her. Following the course of his gaze, she saw Clayt and Melody Carson walking past with their two little boys.

"The Carsons have three kids," Sky said, "holy terrors every one. They're rambunctious, ornery one minute, angelic when it suits them and too smart for their own good. Haley, the oldest put Clayt through the wringer when she first came to live with him, and the other two will probably do the same thing in a couple of years. But when it comes right down to it, I'm pretty sure they're going to be all right. A big reason is that they belong, and they know it."

This wasn't the first Meredith had heard something about a girl named Haley. It seemed to Meredith that Haley was the name of the girl Olivia claimed Logan had tried to kiss. She doubted she had to do with the actual point Sky was trying to make. "Do you belong here, Sky?"

He met her gaze briefly. "As much as I belong anywhere, I guess."

"But you weren't born here."

"What makes you say that?"

"Oh, I don't know." Being careful to keep her tone conversational, she said, "I haven't met anyone else who looks like you, for one thing. Oh, you dress like all the other men, from the faded jeans to the dusty cowboy boots. But black hair and green eyes are an unusual combination.

And you're the only man I've met who takes his hat off in the presence of a lady. Tell me, did you learn that from your father?''

His answer had a lot in common with a snort.

''Your mother?''

He followed his second snort up with a long silence, which he finally broke with a deep sigh. ''Lauralee Larsen.''

Meredith didn't recognize that name, either. ''A friend of yours?'' she asked.

A smile spread across Sky's face. ''She's the one who taught me to take my hat off when I entered a room. Other than you, she's the only woman I've ever considered marrying.''

That he was really considering marrying *her* sent a dozen questions scrambling through her head. But this wasn't about her. It was about him. ''Why didn't you? Marry her, I mean.''

''I don't think she took my marriage proposal seriously.''

Meredith studied Sky. He was being secretive. She couldn't tell if it was intentional. His face was made of strong lines and interesting hollows. His skin was tan, his eyebrows as dark as his hair. But his eyes themselves held a faraway glint that made her want to be let in on the secret.

''Why wouldn't she have taken your proposal seriously?''

He lifted one shoulder in an offhand shrug. ''She probably thought I was too young.''

''Were you?''

''I've always been extremely mature for my age.''

''How old were you?''

''Oh, I don't know. Let's see. That was the year my

mother followed her latest boyfriend to Colorado. Guess I was around eleven. Twelve, maybe. Like I said, I was extremely mature for my age."

"No doubt." Meredith smiled in spite of herself. "You were eleven or twelve the last time you asked a girl to marry you?"

"Lauralee wasn't a girl. She was a woman."

"What was she? Thirteen?"

"Way older than that."

He must have been mature for his age. "Was it love at first sight?"

"It was like at first sight. I didn't fall in love with her until weeks later when she broke up a fight between me and a kid the size of Paul Bunyon who'd called me Redskin just before he plucked my cowboy hat off my head and stomped on it. The hat, that is. If she would have given me five more minutes, I would have had him pulverized. I told Miss Larsen so, too. She made the kid apologize for the racial slur. I told him what he could do with his apology. All I wanted was my hat. I'd saved all summer for it. Thought it would make me fit in. It was about the only thing in the world that meant anything to me."

There was so much information in that one brief explanation that Meredith decided to store most of it for later when she had the time to give it the attention it needed. "You called your Lauralee Larsen, Miss Larsen? You had a crush on your teacher?"

"If you'd seen her, you'd know it was more than a simple crush."

Meredith's smile grew in direct proportion to the all-male glint in Sky's eyes. "Pretty was she?"

He made a sound in the back of his throat only another man could emulate. "Blond hair down to here, a chest out to here, and skin that smelled like roses."

For reasons she couldn't fathom, Meredith was glad Miss Larsen had been blond. "You couldn't convince her to wait for you?"

"She became engaged to somebody else the following spring."

"Who? Someone in high school?"

If he'd heard the faint ribbing in her voice, he ignored it. "Mr. Matthews, the eighth grade science teacher. The guy was old. Practically thirty. He had thin hair and thick glasses. He was probably blind and bald by the time he turned forty."

"There's obviously no accounting for taste."

"That's what I thought."

The smile they shared warmed Meredith's heart. "What did you do?" she asked.

"What makes you think I did anything?"

He'd loosened his grip on his cowboy hat. Tucking the paper bag under her arm, she slipped the Stetson from his grasp. Carefully, she smoothed out the new creases, then handed it back to him. "Call it a sneaking suspicion."

"If you must know, I let the air out of his tires every day for a week. I'd probably still be doing it if he hadn't caught me."

"Oh, dear. He caught you?"

Sky nodded somberly. "He wanted to haul my butt to the principal's office and have me expelled. Miss Larsen wouldn't let him. She worked out a deal. As long as I cut his grass and washed his car, he would let the other incidents go. I cut his grass the next weekend. Miss Larsen showed up when I was washing his car. She helped me finish. By the time we were done, there wasn't a spec on it. Mr. Matthews didn't even notice. I think she knew right then that she'd made the wrong choice."

Meredith laughed out loud. After a time, Sky laughed,

too. Slowly, his laughter trailed away. "We seem to have gotten off the subject."

They also seemed to have moved closer. "What subject is that?" she whispered.

His gaze delved hers before trailing to her mouth. A muscle worked in his jaw. Had he taken another step closer? Or had she?

"You're a complication I hadn't planned on," he said.

As one moment of silence stretched to two, Meredith tried to decide how she felt about being referred to as a complication. Sky wanted her. That much she was sure of. She wanted him, too, just as she had the night the child growing inside her had been conceived. Thoughts of her child brought her back to her senses.

"I didn't plan any of this either, Sky. It's confusing, I know."

"It isn't really that confusing. You're pregnant. It's possible it's my child. We probably should get married for the kid's sake. After all, childhood is hard enough on a kid in the best of circumstances."

Meredith took a backward step. The paper bag Sky had given her when he'd first arrived crumpled, reminding her that she had it. She opened the bag, and withdrew a bra she hadn't seen in two weeks.

"I found it under my bed right after you left that night," he said quietly. "I've been carrying it around in my glovebox since the following morning."

"In your glove box?"

He nodded. "I didn't want to have to try to come up with an explanation in case one of the cowhands found it in my room. A woman's reputation is a delicate thing."

A lump came and went in Meredith's throat. Sky had been protecting her reputation. The area around her heart was slowly but surely turning to mush. This was the third marriage proposal she'd received since word of her pregnancy had spread through Jasper Gulch. So far, Ben Jacobs' "Hey, Mer'dith, whudaya say we get hitched" was the most romantic of the three. However, it wasn't the most sincere.

Returning the undergarment to the bag, she took another backward step. "I don't know what to say."

"Yes comes to mind."

"I don't think we know each other well enough to get married."

"We didn't know each other well enough to fall into bed together, either, but that didn't stop us. I'm trying to do the right thing here, Meredith."

"The right thing for the baby," she said quietly.

He nodded after a time, as if he thought it was odd that she'd felt the need to clarify. "The only thing worse than people speculating about the identity of a kid's father," he said, "is the kid speculating about it."

Only someone who'd experienced a less than satisfactory childhood could make such a statement. Her childhood hadn't exactly been idyllic, either. In fact, she'd spent most of her first fifteen years trying to get out of her childhood, and the better part of the last fourteen years trying to get over it. She wanted so much more for this child. But marriage? She couldn't believe she was even considering it. "I need time to think about this, Sky."

"The sooner we get married, the sooner folks will forget how many months there were between the wedding and the birth." He must have read her look of utter dismay, because he said, "It's true. Haven't you ever heard people say that second babies take nine months, but the first one can come anytime? If that baby's mine, I'd just as soon give him my name right from the start."

Him? "What makes you think this baby will be a boy?"

He glanced away, as if considering the question. When he next met her gaze, his eyes were as steady as his voice. "It doesn't matter whether it's a boy or a girl. If it's mine, I'd want the child to have my name, regardless."

If.

It was amazing how a word so small could be so significant. In her heart, Meredith believed that Sky thought he was doing the right thing. He wanted what was best for this child. If the baby was his, he'd said. If, if, if.

It occurred to her that he was looking at her, an expectant expression on his face. "You want an answer right now?" she asked.

He graced her with his slow, disarming smile. "I don't mean to rush you. It's just that if this child's mine, I'd like to get started giving him," he eyed her knowingly, "or her a stable childhood."

There was that word again. If. "Did you have much stability when you were a child?"

"I had a roof over my head."

Meredith read as much between those lines as she had in the entire tale about Miss Lauralee Larsen. Childhood was supposed to be the happiest time of a person's life. Neither hers nor Sky's had been carefree.

Behind them, the mother cat got her feet underneath her then stood. The two kittens that weren't finished eating meowed forlornly. Peaches, the mother cat, started for the three-sided drawer Logan had padded with an old rug. She looked back once, and meowed twice. All seven of her kittens started toward her on wobbly legs. She waited until they were all safely in the drawer, then busily began the task of cleaning seven coats. Meredith didn't know how animals coped with so many offspring. She was having a hard time making the right choices for one.

And she so wanted to make the right decision for her

child. She couldn't do that without careful deliberation. "I really am going to need a little time to think about this, Sky."

"How long?"

She very nearly pulled a face. "I'm not sure. I'll let you know as soon as I've decided. I promise."

He stared into her eyes for interminable seconds. "All right. You go ahead and think. You know where to find me." With a nod, he turned on his heel. Fitting his hat to his head as if it were second nature, he ambled away as quietly as he had arrived.

Meredith thought about Sky's proposal all afternoon. She thought about it when she wasn't waiting on customers and while she tackled that reupholstering job she'd taken on for that sweet Cletus McCully. The kindly old man had said he was in no hurry. It was a good thing, because Meredith did more thinking than cutting or pinning or stitching. She thought about it while she prepared a wholesome kettle of homemade vegetable soup for her supper, and later, while she locked the store and climbed the stairs to her apartment yet again. She even thought about it while she was in the shower, and after, when she studied her body in the mirror, looking for changes that would indicate that a baby was indeed growing within her. She grinned like an idiot simply because already, there were a few. Her stomach wasn't as flat as it had been, and tomorrow she would have to go shopping for a new bra.

That reminded her of the bra Sky had returned earlier that afternoon. He'd put it in a plain brown wrapper to protect her reputation. He really was a gentleman. She made a face into the mirror. So he wasn't an ax murderer. So what? That didn't mean she should marry him. Or should she?

By the time she'd crawled into bed, she realized she was no longer just thinking about Sky's marriage proposal. She was thinking about Sky. Kids loved him. Horses loved him. Jake and Josie McKenna loved him. Skyler Buchanan was a sincere, secretive man who brought out yearnings and feelings she didn't necessarily want to feel. She didn't know what to do about them. She didn't know what to do about him.

By the following morning, she'd thought about him so much that her head had begun to swim. Raising her hand to knock on Josie McKenna's front door at a quarter past ten, Meredith didn't think that thinking was helping all that much. She simply did not know what to do.

While she waited patiently for her knock to be answered, she listed all the things she knew for sure. There was a baby, a mother, a father, a strong attraction, and a marriage proposal. She liked Sky, and she was pretty sure he liked her. Something was missing. He was a good man. She'd sensed that the first time she'd met him. How many men would propose marriage without being sure of the child's paternity?

Raising her hand to knock a second time, Meredith knew what was missing. Trust. Sky wanted to do the right thing, if the baby was his. If.

When her second knock went unanswered, she chided herself for not calling first. Shuffling the accent pillows and lace panels into her other arm, she strolled to the top step on the McKenna's wraparound porch. Flowers bloomed in beds all along the porch, in pots on the steps, and in the window boxes Jake had had installed for his new wife. A half-grown brown puppy looked up at her forlornly from a pen well away from the flower beds that, upon closer inspection, showed definite signs of digging. Someone had mentioned that the Lone M was the second largest spread in the area. It certainly looked vast to Meredith. It also looked well tended. The fences were straight and stretched as far as the eye could see. Most of the outbuildings had metal roofs. Only the bunkhouse roof was made of old cedar shakes.

A movement out in the corral drew her gaze. Five-year-old Kelsey McKenna was perched in front of Sky on a gentle-looking, medium-sized white horse. "Miz Warner, look at me."

Shading her eyes with one hand, Meredith started down the steps. One of Sky's arms was wrapped firmly around the girl's waist. His other hand hovered inches away from the reins, which were grasped tightly in Kelsey's hands.

Meredith said, "It looks like you're learning to ride, Kelsey."

The child nodded so hard her hair fell into her face. "Sky says I'm still too little to ride alone, but he's teaching me for later. Mama's not home. Where's Olivia?"

"She and Logan went into Pierre with Wes and Jayne to see a man about a horse."

Meredith smiled to herself at the memory of Olivia putting it that way. Both of those kids had a penchant for making her smile. Thanks to them, she was learning a lot about children. For instance, she knew that as long as the different foods on a plate didn't touch each other, they were edible, and red suckers tasted better than green, and a child didn't have to go anywhere near dirt to get dirty. Last but not least, she knew that it simply wasn't in a five-year-old child's makeup to keep a secret for more than two minutes.

She stopped at her car, where she deposited the pillows and curtains she'd intended to show Josie, then headed across the driveway once again. She strolled to the gate, and leaned against it, her hands resting on the top board, one foot on the bottom one.

Kelsey grinned at Meredith as the horse and its riders loped past, but Sky kept his eyes downcast and his voice steady as he talked Kelsey through her lesson. The second time around, Kelsey said, "We hafta keep Louie in her pen, on account'a she's still just a puppy and she might spook old Nellie."

"I think that's a good idea, Kelsey," Meredith said.

The third time around, Kelsey blew a shock of red hair out of her face. Growing serious, she said, "I can't talk no more, Miz Warner. Sky says I'm s'posed to consecrate."

Sky chose that moment to glance at Meredith, his gaze meeting hers beneath the brim of his brown hat. Meredith felt as if the wind had been knocked out of her. The next time around, Kelsey waved by wiggling her fingers and nothing else. Sky smiled. Meredith returned Kelsey's wave and did her best to return Sky's grin. It wasn't easy, because something intense flared through her, something she wasn't sure she'd ever felt in exactly this way. She couldn't even blame it on all the thinking she'd been doing, because suddenly she couldn't seem to put two thoughts together in her head.

There was something mesmerizing about the gentleness in the big hand wrapped protectively around Kelsey's waist, something hypnotic about the low murmur of his voice. *I could fall in love with him.* The thought left her warm and wanting in both mind and spirit, and scared her at the same time, because that was something else that had been lacking in Sky's marriage proposal. Love. He didn't trust her enough to believe the baby was his. And he didn't love her.

Suddenly, she understood why all her thinking had led

her nowhere. All the thinking, all the analyzing of all the reasons she had for marrying him couldn't make up for what was lacking. The fact that he was gentle with creatures big and small couldn't take the place of love and trust.

Gravel crunched in the distance. A moment later, a car pulled into the Lone M's long driveway. One of the ranch trucks tooled in right behind it. "Mama's home!" Kelsey said. "And Buck and Billy, too."

"Whoa," Sky murmured, to Kelsey or to the horse, Meredith couldn't tell. He dismounted with an agility and ease that made him seem weightless, then reached up for Kelsey. "You're a natural-born rider," he said, setting the girl on the fence near Meredith.

Kelsey clapped her hands and scampered down the other side of the fence. "Wait'll I tell Mama."

Meredith glanced over her shoulder, watching as Kelsey ran toward the house, her feet pumping, her red hair flying behind her. Sky watched her, too. About the time the child reached her mother, the wind blew Josie's loose fitting dress against her body, accentuating the rounding of her stomach that resembled the shape of a basketball. Meredith could hardly wait until she looked like that.

"Other than her red hair, Josie says Kelsey looks like her late husband," Sky said. "I wonder if the next baby will look like Jake."

Something in the tone of his voice drew Meredith around. "Not all children look like their father, Sky."

The horse nudged Sky's shoulder with her big head. The gentle hand Sky placed on the animal's broad muzzle was at odds with the tone of his voice as he said, "You think I don't know that?"

The sound of an approaching vehicle kept her from answering. The car had stopped near the house, but the pickup truck loaded high with bales continued in their direction, pulling to a stop near them. "Hey, Sky," Buck Matthews said through the open window.

The other ranch hand called, "Mornin' Mer'dith. You come out to take a look at Sky's place so you can get started on the redecoratin'?"

"Actually, I..."

"Yes, she did," Sky said, droning out Meredith's quieter voice.

Sky felt Meredith's eyes on him. Buck and Billy's, too, for that matter. He looped old Nellie's reins around the top board, then scaled the fence in one, smooth motion. It was either do that, or remain facing the young cowhands, who were bound to notice the results of the zing that had gone through him the moment he'd first noticed Meredith on the front porch. There was nothing overtly sexy about her white slacks and sleeveless red shirt. Until the wind fluttered through it, that is.

Placing his hands over his head in a stretch he hoped looked more casual than it felt, Sky asked the cowhands to take the mare inside, then gestured toward the bunkhouse a hundred yards away. He kept a respectable distance between him and Meredith as they headed that way. Holding the door for her, he berated himself for the quick whiff he took as she walked by. Mmmm. Peaches and sunshine. He was thirty years old. That should have been plenty old enough to control his lust. It was difficult enough to do in public. Now that he had her to himself in the privacy of his place, it was next to impossible.

Meredith seemed to be having no such trouble. She'd strolled around to the back of the sofa, and was gliding her hand over the worn fabric. "What colors do you like, Sky? Navy? Forest green, perhaps?"

"Surprise me." He'd spoken more brusquely than he'd intended.

Her gaze delved his, and she squared her shoulders. "Would you tell me something?"

"I'll try."

"Who do you look like?"

The question took him by surprise. "I've been told there's some Apache in my blood. Somewhere."

Meredith studied Sky. He hadn't removed his hat. Maybe he'd left it on because he was home. Or maybe he didn't want her to see whatever emotion was glittering in his eyes. His skin was tan, his hair dark. She remembered when he'd mentioned some kid who'd called him redskin, but she hadn't been referring to that. She wondered if his vague reference had been intentional. "I meant who do you look like? Your mother? Or your father?"

"Not my mother, that's for sure."

Meredith sauntered a little closer. For heaven's sakes, it was like pulling teeth. "Your father, then?"

"You worried the kid will be ugly?"

She had to force herself to close her gaping mouth. Ugly? The thought hadn't entered her mind. Now that he mentioned it, she realized she didn't care what the baby looked like. She loved this child. Looks weren't going to change that.

"Why?" she asked, playing along. "Was your father ugly?"

He settled his hands on his hips and took an audible breath. "Look. My mother's maiden name was Buchanan. When I was growing up, she gave me a different story and a different name every time I asked about my dad. I'm pretty sure my father, and I use the term loosely, is a man named Hank Nichols. When he isn't shacking up with some woman, he lives in a run-down trailer on the outskirts of San Antonio. He has black hair and green eyes, and no, I guess he isn't ugly, at least not on the outside.''

Meredith didn't know how to proceed. A few things about Skyler Buchanan were becoming clear. It seemed he had good reason for his lack of trust in a woman's word. He'd suffered as a result of his childhood, and he didn't like the thought of his child going through what he'd gone through. If it was his, that is.

"Well?" he asked. "Do you have any more questions?"

Her head pounded, and her stomach felt queasy. It had more to do with Sky's attitude than morning sickness. She wished she had more time to prepare what she had to say, but Sky was waiting for her answer. "It doesn't sound as if you had a great childhood, Lauralee Larsen notwithstanding.''

His lips relaxed a little. "I lived through it. I'd just as soon any kid of mine didn't have to say the same someday.''

"It's not that simple, Sky. My childhood was less than idyllic, too. My father married my mother because she was pregnant. Having two kids didn't exactly make the marriage work. He took off right after I was born.''

"What are you saying?"

She borrowed a gesture from Kelsey, and blew her hair off her forehead. "I'm saying that two people need more than a child between them to make a marriage work.''

"Then your answer is no."

Before she could respond, a knock sounded on the screen door. "Hey, Sky?" one of the ranch hands said through the screen.

"Yeah, Billy?"

The young man opened the door and walked inside. "I hate to bother you, but Jed Harley just called. Seems the

herd we moved over to the west pasture got bored and
took out a section of fence. Several of them are blocking
traffic on Old Stump Road. Want me and Buck to ride
over there?''

"No. I'll go.''

Billy's gaze darted from Meredith to Sky. "You sure?
Cuz it's no trouble.''

"I'm sure. You and Buck can finish unloading the truck.
Meredith and I were finished, anyway.''

Leaving her to read whatever she wanted into that pro-
found statement, he strode out the door without so much
as a backward glance. Meredith said goodbye to Billy.
Pushing her hair behind her ears, she retraced her footsteps
to her car. After retrieving the items she'd stacked there
earlier, she continued on to the porch. This time Josie
opened the door as soon as Meredith knocked.

In the barn, Billy Schmidt lifted the saddle off old Nellie's back and heaved it onto the rack. At twenty-two, he
was a good ranch hand. Sky knew he was saving every
dime to buy a ranching operation some day. His eye for
detail was going to come in handy when he had his own
place. Opening the door to Bommer's stall, Sky could have
done without the younger man's scrutiny today.

"If you wanna wait a coupl'a minutes, me'n Buck'll
have the truck unloaded so you can take it out to Jed's
place.''

Sky had winked a million times in his life. Today, it
practically cracked his face. Running a hand down Bommer's neck, he said, "There are some places trucks can't
go. Besides, Bommer's itching for a good run. Aren't you
boy?''

The beautiful animal tossed his head and pawed at the
floor. Bommer's excitement was contagious. Sky's chuckle
felt more natural as he led the horse to the open area in

the tack room. On the other side of a shoulder-high wall, Buck and Billy began unloading bales of straw from the bed of the truck. Sky prepared Bommer for the saddle, only half listening to the ranch hands banter.

"You doin' anything this weekend?"

"Don't know what I'll do Friday, but I'll probably end up going to the dance at the town hall to listen to the Anderson Brothers play Saturday night."

"Me, too. Ya know, if those boys would spend half as much time thinking about ranching as they do thinking about music, they'd have a successful operation out there."

Their voices came and went, and Sky knew they were traipsing back and forth from the truck to the area where they were stacking the bales of straw. They were good workers, those two.

"I hear Neil's been spending a lot of time at the new gal's paint and furniture store."

"Yeah, I heard that, too."

"Far as I know, he ain't fixin' to paint his place."

On the other side of the wall, Sky paused.

"What do you suppose he's doing there?"

"I dunno. Maybe he likes her. She is a looker."

"That's for sure. Think it's possible Mer'dith's baby's gonna be musically inclined?"

The implication hit Sky between the eyes. He tightened the cinch, adjusted the stirrups, then swung onto Bommer's strong back. He ducked under the barn door, then urged Bommer through the gate he'd already opened. Man and horse raced down the lane, the wind in their faces. No matter how fast they ran, Sky couldn't outrun the dread that sat like a brick in his stomach.

Speculation had begun.

* * *

Meredith was walking out the door when she heard the sound of thundering hoofbeats. Josie and Kelsey strode to the porch railing, where all three of them shaded their eyes with their hands.

"There he goes again," Kelsey exclaimed dramatically.

"Again?" Meredith asked.

"Sky's an enigma," Josie said. "He's got so much life in him, so much goodness. But sometimes he rides his horse too fast, and drives the same way. Jake says he's always done that. In a couple of days, he'll take the jeep and hightail it out of here."

"He just up and leaves?" Meredith asked.

Josie and her little girl both nodded.

"He's a free spirit," Josie said matter-of-factly.

And Kelsey quipped, "But he always comes back, right Mama?"

"That's right, sweet pea."

An enigma, yes, but a free spirit? Meredith wouldn't have described him in quite that way. "Where does he go?" she asked.

Josie shrugged. "I don't know if Jake's ever asked. Jake and Sky are like that. It's a guy thing."

The conversation turned to other things. When Meredith said she had to get back to the store, Josie and Kelsey went back inside, and Meredith returned to her car and drove home.

Sky was going to leave the ranch in a few days? Where did he go? Why did he go?

And why didn't anyone around here bother to ask?

Chapter Seven

It was nine in the morning when Meredith pulled into the long dusty driveway that led to the bunkhouse where Sky lived. Already, the temperature was nearly eighty degrees, the sky the lightest blue she'd ever seen. Three horses watched from the corral, and somewhere, a calf bawled forlornly. Parking her car near the bunkhouse, she got out. Other than an occasional clunk and bang coming from one of the sheds, and the half-grown puppy that yipped from the front porch of the main house closer to the road, there didn't appear to be much activity in and around the Lone M this morning.

The sun shone through the curtainless window on the east side of the bunkhouse, lighting up the inside of the rustic structure. Nothing moved. The place looked deserted, the windows and door closed up tight.

"Well," she said to the teenage girls she'd hired. "Might as well knock and see if anybody's home."

She wasn't surprised when her knock went unanswered

a few moments later. Sharla Avery, the older of the two girls, said, "Think we should have called first?"

Meredith shook her head. "Sky doesn't have a phone."

"Ugh, that's right," the petite brunette exclaimed. "How can anyone survive without a phone?"

"Sky's a free spirit," Holly Quinn, the other girl said matter-of-factly. "I guess free spirits don't need to make phone calls."

"I saw that dreamy Billy Schmidt's truck over by the shed," Sharla said. "If you want, I'll go ask him if he knows where Sky went."

"Sky isn't here."

The deep, male voice had come from someplace directly behind them. Meredith, Holly and Sharla all turned around; poor Sharla was the only one who turned slightly red.

"Billy!"

"Hey, Sharla," Billy Schmidt said, a twinkle in his eyes and a smile on his face.

In an effort to give the girl a few seconds to recover, Meredith smiled at the handsome young cowhand she'd seen a few days ago, and said, "Do you know where Sky went?"

"Me and Buck half expected him to be gone when we got up this morning, but he wasn't."

"He isn't gone?"

"Well, he's gone, but he isn't gone-gone. He and Buck are mending fences over by Old Stump Road. I had to help Slappy get the carburetor out of the tractor. Now I'm heading out there, myself." Billy flashed a smile at Sharla. "You plannin' to go to the dance Saturday night?"

"What time?" Sharla was fresh out of high school. For once, she seemed to be fresh out of feminine wiles. Closing her eyes, she all but groaned out loud. "I mean, I might."

Billy's grin spread across his face. "I could pick you up around eight."

"Eight sounds good."

He slanted Sharla another one of his dreamy smiles, asked Holly about her father, then looked at Meredith. "You fixin' to surprise Sky, like he said?"

Meredith hadn't planned to do that, but she considered it now. "Maybe I will," she answered.

"Then I won't tell him I saw you." Angling Sharla another of his dreamy smiles, he gave the brim of his hat a slight tug, turned on his heel and ambled away on footsteps so silent it was no wonder they hadn't heard his approach.

Holly opened the bunkhouse door, and the two girls walked in, the epitome of quiet dignity, only to burst into giggles the second they were inside. "I can't believe he heard me say that!" Sharla exclaimed.

"He likes you," Holly insisted.

"I know."

Both girls stopped suddenly, peering all around. "Wow," Sharla exclaimed. "And my mom thinks my room is a mess. Looks like we have our work cut out for us."

"I guess free spirits don't mind a little clutter," Holly stated.

Meredith eyed some of Sky's things, and then her new employees. Both girls wore cutoffs and cowboy boots. The similarities stopped there. Although Sharla was older, Holly was already taller. And Sharla's face didn't bear the telltale signs of sadness.

People here liked to talk. In that respect, they were no different than people anywhere. They dropped names into conversations along with snippets of history. For instance, someone had told Meredith that Sharla's great-great-great-grandfather had been the first doctor to settle out here. More than one person had mentioned that Holly's dear mother had died six months ago following a nasty fight with cancer. Everyone in Jasper Gulch seemed to expect Sky to leave town any second, even these two teenage girls.

"You're not the first people I've heard refer to Sky as a free spirit. Why do folks around here call him that?"

Sharla didn't have to think about her answer. "Because he comes and goes as he pleases, for one thing."

"My dad says that sometimes, late at night, Sky races the wind," Holly added. Her voice had been quieter, more thoughtful, as if she knew how it felt to want to race the wind after midnight.

Meredith's heart went out to the girl. Sadness had dulled Holly's eyes and dampened her spirit. Hopefully, this summer job would help ease her loneliness and help time pass while her heart mended.

"Where do we start?" Holly asked, as if itching to get busy.

Meredith would have liked to ask more questions about Sky. Instead, she fastened her hair at her nape with a wide elastic band, and said, "I guess we start by hauling all this stuff out, and our paint and supplies in."

The girls began carting the smaller pieces of furniture outside, and Meredith began stacking old newspapers and junk mail on a pile. An unopened envelope caught her attention. It appeared to be from an attorney and had been postmarked in a place called Box Elder.

Trying for nonchalance, she said, "Either of you ever hear of a town called Box Elder?"

Holly and Sharla took turns shrugging and shaking their heads. In the end, they both agreed that the town sounded familiar, but they didn't know where it was. Sharla even went so far as to say, "It's probably just another small town like a hundred other small towns in South Dakota. Why?"

"I'm new around here, and I just wondered," Meredith answered.

Seemingly satisfied, the girls went back to work. Before long, the room was nearly empty, and Holly and Sharla were talking about boys and dances and the clothes they would spend their first paychecks on. Meredith only half listened. The rest of her mind was on Sky. She wondered if he attended town dances. While she was at it, she wondered why so many people who'd known him for years automatically assumed he was a free spirit, when Meredith didn't see him that way at all.

Who did he know in Box Elder? Where was Box Elder? And why had he left such an official looking letter unopened? She wondered that most of all.

Sky felt the vibration of dozens of boots stomping the floor the moment he set foot inside the town hall. He'd heard the music long before he'd inched into a parking spot two blocks away from the town hall. Now that he was here, he understood why folks were talking about all the time the Anderson boys spent practicing their music instead of minding the ranch. For years, Neil, Ned and Norbert had played at weddings, town picnics, the yearly Fourth of July barbecue. Lately, they'd taken to hosting a dance every chance they got. Their outlooks had been gloomy for months. They sure seemed to be enjoying themselves tonight.

Glancing around, Sky noticed that they weren't the only ones having a good time. The place was crowded. The town hall had been getting a lot more use since the local boys had decided to advertise for women to come to Jasper

Gulch a couple of years back. Most of the women who'd answered that ad were now happily married. Several of them were on the dance floor right now. Truth be told, it wasn't one of the married gals he was looking for.

"Hey Sky," Billy Schmidt said on his way to the punch table with Paul and Sherry Avery's youngest daughter.

"Hi Billy," Sky replied.

"Those boys sure can strum a tune," one of the other area ranchers said.

Figuring this was as good a place to stand as any, Sky exchanged a few words with the small group of men he'd known for years. "The boys sound good tonight."

"I heard Neil's gonna make an announcement tonight," Boomer Brown said.

"I heard that, too," Jed Harley added.

Sky hadn't, but then, he'd spent the last three days on the range, and hadn't heard much of anything other than the bawl of cattle and the sigh of the wind. Just then, the crowd parted, and Sky got his first glimpse of Meredith across the room. He wasn't the only man in the room watching her, but since there wasn't any law against looking, he could hardly fault the local boys for enjoying the view.

Small white lights were strung in the rafters. The only other illumination came from more than a dozen antique wall sconces lining the room. The dim bulbs cast shadows in the corners, fading colors much the way moonlight did. Meredith's hair shimmered, long and straight down her back, swaying slightly as she danced with first one, and then another of the Jasper Gents.

"She's a hard one to figure out," someone said behind Sky.

"That, she is," someone else agreed.

Sky rested his hands on his hips, redistributed his weight to one foot and simply watched.

"Maybe," Boomer said. "But she's also a hard gal not to like. DoraLee is amazed that folks haven't given her a harder time than they have, and frankly, so am I. A couple of the old hens in the Ladies Aid Society had a cow about the fact that Meredith is gonna have a baby but isn't gonna get married, but even they are having a hard time coming up with much gossip about her."

"It's like Boomer said," Jed agreed, "She's a hard gal not to like."

"She's got class."

"And taste."

"She turned Keith Gurski and Clive Hendricks down cold. See that?" Ben Jacobs said. "She even keeps Rory O'Grady at arm's length, and everybody knows he's got a way with women."

A smug feeling of satisfaction settled over Sky. His estimation of Meredith had gone up a notch when he wasn't looking. He still didn't know where he stood on the issue of paternity, but Meredith had been true to her word. There *had* been some speculation about her, but he had yet to hear that she'd dropped his, or anyone else's name in connection to her pregnancy.

One song ended and another began. As the men shuffled off the dance floor, more women flocked onto it, forming three lines. Meredith wound up in the middle of the front row, stepping into a country line dance. She sure was easy on the eyes. She was wearing a blue dress he'd seen before. Loose fitting, it buttoned down the front, and twirled around her legs as she moved. Most women out here wore cowboy boots to local dances. Meredith wore leather shoes with clunky little heels that made her ankles look unbelievably delicate. The soles must have been slippery, because she slid through the sawdust someone had sprinkled on the floor. Laughing at the woman who was showing her the steps, she tried again.

She'd made friends here. And not just with the local bachelors, although they'd fallen all over themselves to get her attention. Meredith talked to the women, too. In fact, she and that genius Crystal Galloway were whooping it up as if they'd been friends forever.

"Hey, Sky," one of the few red-haired ranch hands in town said. "Has Meredith been out to your place to work her magic yet?"

There was a noticeable shift in the beating rhythm of Sky's heart, a slight catch in his breathing. "Her magic?" he asked without taking his eyes off Meredith.

"You took first place in that naming contest, didn't you?"

Oh, that magic. "Yeah. She came out to the bunkhouse while I was out on the range. I don't know how she did it. It looks like my place, only better."

It was true. There was nothing fussy about the room, but there was a coziness that hadn't been there before. The old plank floor had been painted a dark cinnamon color, the walls several shades lighter. She'd left the pegged hat rack by the door. Other than the new throw draped over the back of his couch, most of the items in the room were things that had been lying around for years. The old lantern that had sat on the floor in the corner now sat on a shelf made out of old barn wood. An antique picture of a man and his horse racing down a path now hung on one wall. And she'd hung a horseshoe over his door, its ends pointing to the ceiling to keep the luck from running out.

"She thought of everything," he said.

"Too bad there aren't more single women like her in

this neck of the woods. There's just something about a woman's touch.''

There was something about *Meredith's* touch, Sky thought. He'd been on the range for three days, and ached in all the usual places. Watching Meredith be herself tonight—friendly and outgoing—made him realize that he'd been unkind to her. And he'd had no right.

Sky didn't remember making his way to the other side of the room. Once he was there, how he'd gotten there didn't matter. The song had ended, the dance floor had cleared. He took advantage of the relative quiet to murmur, ''Hello, Meredith.''

She raised her eyes to his and wavered him a woman-soft smile that went straight to his head. The first notes of a slow song strummed to life around them. While she took a deep breath, Sky held his. ''Care to dance?'' he finally asked.

Meredith's heart was beating wildly. She knew it was more than the last dance. It had to do with Sky. She'd danced with a dozen men tonight. None of them had this effect on her. She and Sky shared an intense physical awareness. Her mind told her to resist. The rest of her didn't listen, and she found herself nodding, and placing her hand in his. He turned her into his arms in the center of the dance floor. She closed her eyes, thinking how easy it would be to lean against him. Calling on an inner strength that had taken years to cultivate, she kept a respectable distance between them and said, ''How do you like your place?''

''It smells good. Like you,'' he answered, close to her ear.

If he noticed that she'd straightened her back in an effort to keep from melting into him, he didn't comment. Instead, he led her in a simple two-step, and she followed.

"Have you been here long?" she asked.

"Long enough to see you dance with nearly every single man between the ages of eighteen and eighty."

"I didn't do anything for them I haven't done for you." Realizing how that sounded, she forgave him for the way his muscles bunched beneath her hand. "I was referring to dancing, Sky."

"I know, Meredith. I guess it isn't your fault that I can't seem to forget the night we met." She was considering that when he said, "They like you."

She peered over his shoulder at the other couples on the floor, and all the men watching from all around the room. "Single women are outnumbered in this county, that's all."

"And the *Titanic* got a nasty scratch from that iceberg."

A smile found its way to her face. An answering grin found its way to his. He turned her without warning, eliciting a little yelp from her. When he dipped her, she laughed out loud.

Those dancing close turned at the sound of Sky's answering chuckle. Skyler Buchanan had most likely always been light on his feet, so there was nothing unusual about his agile turn in one direction, or his smooth sway in another. Meredith wondered if there was anything unusual about the amorous attention he was paying her.

Somebody tapped him on the shoulder. His steps slowed as he glanced at the man responsible for the intrusion.

Clive Hendricks smiled as if he was letting Sky in on a dirty joke. "Now that you've got her all loosened up, I thought I'd take a turn."

A chill ran up Meredith's spine. At first glance, Clive Hendricks wasn't ugly. But he had a nasty smile, a mean laugh, a dirty leer. Meredith wasn't afraid of him, but she sure didn't like him. "I don't think…"

"Sure you do, sugar," Clive said, easing closer.

Meredith could hardly believe it when Sky struck up a conversation with the other man. "How are you, Clive?"

Sensing victory, Clive's smile grew, and he moved even closer, as if to take Meredith off Sky's hands. Meredith was frantically searching for a way to avoid a confrontation when Sky gave her hand a quick squeeze and said, "You ever get your nose looked at, Clive?"

Clive brought his thick, stubby fingers to the little bump in his nose, a souvenir left over from the night Doc Kincaid broke it defending Louetta Graham's honor last year. "No, why?"

"That's probably wise," Sky answered. "No sense getting it fixed, only to get it broken all over again."

The smile drained from Clive's face like water from a kicked bucket. Clamping his lips together, he took a backward step. Sky and Meredith resumed their dance, or at least Sky did. Meredith simply floated along, her heart in her throat. In his own quiet way, Sky had put Clive in his place. He'd come to her rescue. Not like a knight on a charging white horse. More like a magician who could make something bad disappear with the flick of one finger and a wave of his hand.

No one had ever done that for her before. She'd responded physically to him the first night she saw him. This was different. This was scary.

This was dangerously close to love.

Her footsteps froze right there on the floor.

"Something wrong?" Sky asked, stopping, too.

She nodded. She had to sit down. Swallowing the lump in her throat, she started across the room. She hadn't taken a dozen steps before the song ended. The next thing she knew, Neil Anderson was calling her name over the microphone.

"Folks," Neil said loudly. "I'd like to take a minute to talk to you about something. Meredith, come on up here, darlin'. It's only right that you're in on this."

A murmur went through the crowd. Feeling like a deer trapped in the glare of headlights, Meredith looked at the sea of faces all around her. Resigning herself to this new twist of fate, she pasted a smile on her face, straightened her back, and did as Neil asked.

Sky stalked off the dance floor, alone. If anybody had been looking, they would have noticed the severe expression on his face. But they weren't looking at Skyler Buchanan. They were looking at the woman in blue who was ascending the steps to the stage.

The Anderson brothers grinned at one another as if they had a secret. Sky didn't remember the last time he saw any of them looking so happy. Hell, they looked downright excited. When Neil took Meredith's hand, Sky felt like chewing glass.

"Folks," Neil said. "I have an announcement to make. Now I'm sure you've all noticed that me and the boys, me in particular, have been as grouchy as a bear with a sore paw these past couple of years. It took Meredith here to open my eyes. Some of you boys will be happy to know that there's about to be fewer bachelors in town."

Neil grinned at Meredith. Dread dropped to Sky's stomach.

"Meredith here's made a suggestion, and well, I've decided to take her up on it."

Neil continued talking. Sky had stopped listening, and headed for the door.

Meredith searched the crowd for one rugged, dark-haired man. Neil and his brothers were dear friends, but they had poor timing. She'd just realized that she was falling in love. She wanted to be down there with Sky. Where was he, anyway?

A movement way over by the door caught her eye. It looked as if Sky was leaving. Reaching for the microphone, Meredith said, "The breeze in South Dakota isn't the only thing that's long-winded. What Neil is trying to say is…"

Her voice trailed away as she watched Sky disappear out the door. "On second thought," she said, handing the microphone back to Neil. "It's your news. It's only fitting that you should tell them."

"Where are you going?"

"I need some fresh air. Good night everybody." She hurried down the steps, and practically ran to the door. She paused on the sidewalk to catch her breath. Squinting into the shadows, she saw Sky's dark figure moving away toward a row of cars and trucks stretching all the way to Main Street.

"Going someplace?" she called, going after him.

His steps slowed, but he didn't stop. "I hope you and Neil are very happy."

"What are you talking about?" She looked both ways automatically before crossing the deserted street.

"You're a smart woman. Figure it out. Tell me this. Did you tell Neil he's the father, too?"

"The father? Sky, would you stop walking away and let me think?" Her mind raced, slapping two and two together and haphazardly coming up with four. "Neil's leaving Jasper Gulch, Sky."

"Where are you going?"

"I'm not going anywhere."

That got his attention. And he finally stopped, although he had yet to turn around and face her.

"You know, Sky, for a free spirit, you're awfully closed

off. I moved to Jasper Gulch to be near Logan and Olivia. This is where my family is. This is where my business is." This was where her child's father was. All this hurrying was making her breathless. She stopped a dozen strides away from him, not far from her store. "As I was saying. This is where I want to stay. Unlike me, Neil and Norbert and Ned aren't happy in Jasper Gulch. They don't want to raise corn and cattle. They want to play music. You heard them. You must know how talented they are. Their talents are being wasted here. That's why they're going to Nashville."

Finally, he faced her. "You mean, when Neil called you up on stage, it wasn't to—"

She shook her head.

"He didn't—"

She gave her head another, smaller shake.

"Then you aren't—"

She told herself he didn't deserve her smile. She didn't have it in her to withhold it.

"Well."

"Is that all you have to say, Sky?"

He strode the remaining distance between them, whisked his hat off his head and swooped his hand, hat and all around behind her, drawing her against his body in a motion so smooth and effortless she didn't have time to do more than gasp before his mouth covered hers. He made a sound deep in his throat, part need, all male. And then, with a gentleness she sensed was as much a part of him as his affinity with horses and riding like the wind, he deepened the kiss. Meredith was pretty sure her heart had tipped over, floating gently down to her stomach. Something was beating there, something warm and sinuous and sweet.

The kiss went on and on, pulsing like a ripple on a glass-smooth lake, spreading outward in a pattern that was so beautiful, that when it was over, you wanted to toss in another stone just to experience it all over again. Only Sky didn't kiss her again when it was over. He drew away, an inch at a time. Reaching a hand to her cheek, he ran his thumb along her jaw, his eyes delving hers before fixing on her mouth once again. "For the record," he said, his voice a husky murmur, another slow sweep along her senses.

"Yes?" she whispered.

A muscle worked in his throat, and his voice lowered, deepened much the way his kiss had. "For the record," he repeated, "I'm not closed off."

She couldn't have said a word even if he hadn't slid his fingers across her lips, anymore than she could have taken her eyes off his legendary cowboy swagger as he walked away. He didn't say another word until he reached his truck. "One more thing."

This time, she stood mute and perfectly still.

He opened his door and peered at her over his shoulder. "I'm glad you're not leaving town."

If she lived to be a hundred, she would never forget the feeling that washed over her. It didn't feel dangerous at all. It felt wonderful, like nothing she'd ever felt before.

She expected him to start his truck and drive away. When he didn't, she looked at him quizzically. And he said, "I'd feel better if I knew you'd gotten in safely."

Meredith could have told him that she'd been taking care of herself most of her life. Instead, she reached into her pocket, drew out her key, and let herself into her store. Her legs felt quivery as she went up the long flight of stairs. Unlocking her apartment door, she went inside. She flipped the light on, then strode to the window. She stayed there until Sky had pulled away, and his taillights had disappeared down the street.

So this was love.

She sank into a chair. She'd expected love to resemble a floating sensation. Instead, it felt like a boulder that was rolling precariously close to the edge of a cliff.

"What do you know?" she said, patting her stomach. "I'm in love with your daddy."

She didn't know what she was supposed to do now. She only knew that love changed everything.

Meredith didn't hear from Sky the next day. On Monday, she decided to take a drive out to the Lone M and see him. She loaded up her car with the items she would need to put the finishing touches on Jake and Josie's place. While she was at it, she wanted to add a few more items to Sky's.

It didn't take her long to hang the valance above Josie's kitchen window. Declining her new friend's offer of a cup of tea, Meredith strode out to the bunkhouse.

Again, her knock went unanswered. Sky wasn't home.

The door was unlocked, though. Hefting the basket of fruit in one hand, she went in. She turned in a circle. Taking a moment to admire her handiwork, she placed the basket on the marred wood table. The junk mail she'd stacked on one corner of the table was gone. Only a letter opener and one envelope remained. It lay, face up, its Box Elder postmark plain to read, and was as empty as Sky's house.

She thought about going back over to the big house and asking Josie where Sky had gone. At the last minute, her steps veered in another direction. She ended up in the wide doorway of a machine shed. "Excuse me," she said to the old man stooped over an engine.

"Why?" he asked, "You do somethin' wrong?" Before she could answer, he forged on. "Just look at this here engine. They don't make 'em like they used to, that's for sure. Two days ago, it was all gummed up and worth about as much as a hill of beans. Now, it's as good as new."

She eased closer. It looked like an old engine to her. "You're good at fixing things?" she asked.

"Only things I can't fix are a broken heart and the crack of dawn. I'll get to work on the crack of dawn as soon as I'm finished with this carburetor. Name's Slappy. Slappy Purvis."

"Your name is really Slappy?"

"Actually, my name's Reginald Purvis, but I'll deny it if you tell anybody."

Meredith smiled. The man had a permanent tan, and skin that resembled old leather. He could have been sixty or eighty. She liked him immediately. She didn't mind his gray whiskers, but she could have done without the telltale bulge of chewing tobacco in his cheek. When he spit, her stomach pitched. "Have you seen Sky?" she asked.

Slappy answered without looking up. "He took the truck to town to pick up feed. Nine'll get you ten that when he gets back, he's gonna hightail it out'a here."

"Where will he go?"

"Wherever he pleases, I reckon."

"Have you ever asked him where he goes?"

"Once or twice."

"And?" she prodded.

He looked up at her through bushy white eyebrows. "Sky don't take kindly to interrogation. Can't say as I blame him."

It required a serious conscious effort to refrain from rolling her eyes. Since she knew a dead end when she was staring at one, she gave up and said, "I put a basket of fruit on his table. If you see him, would you tell him I stopped by?''

Slappy muttered something she couldn't quite make out. Returning to her car, she tried to decide what to do. Skyler Buchanan came and went as he pleased. Nobody bothered to ask where he was going or when he would be back. He was the father of her unborn child, and yet there were things about him she didn't understand. These people had known him for years, but they didn't seem to know him any better than she did.

Maybe it was enough for them. It wasn't enough for her. The thought came out of nowhere. Dangerous or not, she loved him. And she wanted to know him better. That had its own set of risks.

Meredith had been taking risks all her life. It had been risky to leave home when she was barely seventeen. It had been risky to leave a secure job in Chicago and move to a town that was barely big enough to show up on a map. She supposed it had been risky to wind up in Sky's bed the night they'd met. Looking back, that had been the biggest risk of all, because that had been a risk to her heart.

Obviously, Sky took risks, too. He rode his horse at breakneck speed, and drove out of town without looking back. And nobody bothered to ask him why.

Rubbing imaginary dirt off her hands, she decided that it was about time somebody gave Skyler Buchanan a run for his money. She'd spent one idyllic night in his arms. Two months later, he'd asked her to marry him. If either of those things didn't give her the right to be inquisitive, what would?

Sharla and Holly were minding the store. Together, they could handle things for the rest of the day. Deciding on a course of action, she drove to the only main road leading out of Jasper Gulch. She backed her car into a secluded little lane she'd noticed a few days ago. Thankful that her car was dark green, thereby blending with the overgrown brush and weeds, she turned off the engine and waited.

She found Box Elder on her road atlas. As far as she could tell, it was a two hour drive due west. According to the index, it wasn't much bigger than Jasper Gulch. She spent an agonizing hour wondering who Sky knew there.

Did he have a wife? A passel of dark-haired, green-eyed children?

She could have done without the doubts and worries that suddenly plagued her. Now, she couldn't do without answers.

Finally, a dusty silver pickup truck sped past her hiding place. Sky was heading west. Waiting until he was nearly out of sight, she started her car, and followed from a safe distance.

Chapter Eight

Meredith couldn't be certain Sky was going to Box Elder. She only knew he was heading west, and Box Elder was west. She did her best to stay far enough behind him so that he wouldn't recognize her car. It wasn't easy, for Sky didn't drive fast, another fallacy, compliments of the very people who thought they knew him.

She lost sight of him when a pickup truck pulling a horse trailer got between them and proceeded to putz along at a teeth clenching thirty-five miles per hour. Just when she was certain Sky had turned off somewhere, she caught sight of his silver truck rounding a curve half a mile ahead.

He hadn't gone far when his brake lights came on. For a moment, she thought he'd spotted her. Then she realized he'd slowed to a crawl in front of the truck stop where they'd first met. Was it possible that he was remembering that night, too? Meredith would never forget it.

The sun was shining this hot, August morning, but that day in May an uncommonly cold, blustery rain had blown in, chilling her to the bone. Looking back, she realized that she'd been cold for days, ever since she'd learned that Kate and Dusty had been killed in a car accident six months earlier. Six months, and she hadn't known. She drove all the way from Minneapolis to Kate's house without sleeping, or eating, or stopping for more than gasoline.

The house had been cold and damp and empty. Especially empty. Dusty and Kate were dead, and Logan and Olivia had gone to live with their godfather on a ranch near a little town called Jasper Gulch. Standing at the kitchen sink, looking out at the rain-soaked swing set, idle now, tears had coursed down Meredith's face, her grief so strong it nearly choked her. She'd waited too long, and now it was too late to reconcile with her only sister.

She'd endured a lot of empty days in her life, but she'd never felt emptiness in quite that way. Eventually, she'd left Kate's house. Standing in the driveway next to the For Sale sign, she'd realized she had nowhere to go, no one to turn to. Rain soaked her hair and ran down her slicker, splashing onto her ankles, wetting her shoes. Finally, she'd crawled back into her car and drove. Where didn't matter. She shivered. Even with the heater blasting, she couldn't get warm. When her hunger pains became unbearable, she pulled into a truck stop. It was late. Other than a tired waitress who doubled as the cook, the only person inside was a man whose moss-green eyes looked as empty as she felt.

Neither she nor the man spoke for a long time. Finally, he said, "There's nothing like a South Dakota spring, is there?" And even though it hurt, she'd smiled. Eventually, he'd pulled his chair over to her table. Darkness had fallen by then, and rain pelted the windows. Sitting across from a man who called himself Sky, warmth flickered inside her, pulsing, shimmering in her chest, slowly radiating outward. The longer they talked, the less lonely, or empty, or cold she felt. She'd heard all the clichés about fate and connections and matches made in heaven, but until that night, she'd never experienced anything that came close to any of those things. It was as if she'd known him, and he, her.

He'd asked her where she was staying. She'd answered, "I don't know. Nowhere, I guess. It doesn't matter."

Seeing that she was in no condition to drive, he'd offered her his place for the night. With no strength in reserve, she couldn't fathom resisting. He'd planned to sleep on the couch, but back at his house, awareness had built, holding the gloom and the cold and the emptiness at bay. She'd sensed his effort to resist, but he must have needed that connection as desperately as she did. For a few brief hours, she'd believed she'd found love in his arms.

Up ahead, Sky's brake lights went off. And Meredith came back to the present. She'd confused love for relief, and release, and tenderness, a mind-boggling attraction, and a night they'd never forget. Whoa. She couldn't forget it. He probably didn't even remember that they'd first met in that particular truck stop. Worse, he might not have cared. More than likely, he'd only slowed down because he'd contemplated stopping for an early lunch. For whatever reason, he drove right on by.

Meredith dropped back even farther. The terrain went from flat, to gently rolling. Sometimes, she saw huge herds of brown cattle and fences that stretched as far as the eye could see. She drove over bridges spanning shallow rivers, past signs for towns with interesting names such as Seven Mile Corner and Buffalo Gap.

Since she could get nauseated or hungry at a moment's notice these days, she never went anywhere unprepared. Nibbling apple slices and sipping tea from a thermos, she listened to one country-and-western song after another.

Once, an eighteen-wheeler got between them. Later, a flat-nosed gray bus blocked her view. She was beginning to wonder just how far Sky planned to drive when the bus turned off and she realized that the highway stretching ahead of her was empty.

She gripped the steering wheel with both hands. Her eyes darted back and forth, searching for a glimpse, a hint of where he'd gone. It had to be luck that made her notice a small sign with an arrow pointing to Box Elder.

Moments after following that arrow, she passed the village limit sign. She'd found the town. Where was Sky?

Like most small towns, Box Elder's downtown area looked sleepy. She drove past a diner, a hardware store, a barbershop, and an insurance office. Several pickup trucks were parked in front of a tavern. Sky's wasn't among them.

She tried the side streets next, driving past well-kept old houses where dogs snoozed in the shade and bicycles rested on kickstands. A group of kids looked up from the game of baseball they were playing in a vacant lot. Spotting a girl and boy manning a lemonade stand on a corner a few streets over, Meredith pulled to the curb and got out.

It felt good to stretch her legs. After paying a dollar for a paper cup of lukewarm lemonade, she smiled at a curly haired boy and girl. "How's business?" she asked.

"Not so hot," the boy answered. "You're our second customer, and we've been sittin' out here for an hour."

That explained the drink's temperature. The little girl smiled beguilingly, revealing several missing teeth.

With a wink, Meredith asked, "Have either of you seen a silver truck go by?"

"You talkin' about Sky's truck?" the boy asked.

"Do you know Sky?"

"He was our first customer!" the little girl exclaimed. "He's over at Grace's house."

Grace's house? Heaviness centered in Meredith's chest. Sky was visiting a woman? Before her throat closed up completely, she said, "Where's Grace's house?"

She had to spend another dollar on warm lemonade before the boy would tell her. Back behind the wheel, she waved to the children, then followed the boy's simple directions.

The house was nothing like she'd expected. It was an old story-and-a-half, with slate siding and a narrow, uninviting front porch. The grass was tall, and the bushes overgrown. There were no dogs snoozing in the shade, no bicycles leaning on their kickstands. So much for her theory that Sky had half a dozen green-eyed children. It didn't look like the house of a kept woman, either. Please, she prayed, getting out of her car, don't let it be the house of a wife.

Her right foot was on the first step when the screen door creaked open, and she came face-to-face with Sky. Outwardly, they both froze. Inside, a hundred intelligent, eloquent thoughts and questions sped through Meredith's mind.

She opened her mouth to voice one of them. "Who's Grace?" She clamped her mouth shut. She wasn't well.

He waited to answer until after he'd stepped onto the porch and closed the screen door. "How do you know about Grace?"

That wasn't an answer. Nevertheless, it sent a dull ache of foreboding through her. "Two children selling lemonade told me."

He grabbed his hat off his head, raked his fingers through his hair, and put his hat back on in slow order.

"There are no secrets in this town. Never have been. Her name was Grace Miller."

"Was?"

"She died."

"She did?" Not only was Meredith not well, but she was daft, too. Sky didn't seem to notice, his gaze on something in the distance. "Was she pretty?"

This time, he looked at her as if she wasn't the only one who was beginning to think she'd lost her marbles. "She was a snappy, nasty, nagging woman who not only viewed the glass as half-empty, but complained about the hard water spots on the outside. If ever there was a name that didn't suit a person, it was my grandmother's."

"Grace was your grandmother?" Her knees wobbled. Grasping the railing, she began to lower to the step.

Sky was there suddenly, his arm sliding around her, helping her sit down. "You okay?"

He released her after she'd taken a seat, and she thought, he really is a gentleman. Looking way up at him, she smiled. "I'm going to have to get some lunch pretty soon. I was afraid Grace was your wife, or perhaps your mistress, and the two of you had a house full of kids."

He lowered his lanky frame to the step next to her. "I decided early on that the Buchanan gene pool would end with me. I never took chances when it came to that."

The look he cast at her stomach was extremely telling. He still didn't believe the baby was his. Why? What could have made him so skeptical? Better, yet, who?

"When did Grace die?" she asked.

"I'd come from her funeral the night we met," he said, his voice a hollow monotone. "She raised me after my mother ran off, and I owed her. I gave her money, kept the roof patched and food in the fridge."

Sky had a knack for releasing a lot of information in

very few words. Meredith had noticed that before. He remembered the night they'd met, too. He didn't seem nearly as glad about that as she was. She glanced at the grass that was going to seed and the overgrown bushes growing wild next to the steps. Choosing her words carefully, she asked, "Do you miss her?"

He made a sound in the back of his throat that ended when he released a loud breath through his lips. "Like I miss the flu."

"It was just the two of you?" she asked. "Your grandma and you?"

He made another disparaging sound. "I never called her grandma. Last I knew, my father, and I use the term loosely, was still alive. I ran away to find him when I was fourteen. Had to go through a long list. My mother's word wasn't exactly golden."

"But you found him?"

"He wasn't worth the trouble, believe me."

"What about your mom?"

"She ran off when I was eight. Grace decided to let me live here. My grandfather died before I was born. Grace's second husband ran off after only a year of wedded bliss. My mother came back a couple of times and dragged me off with her again. Ultimately, she took up with another jerk and ended up putting me on a bus headed back here. At least here I had a room and food on the table. It was better than getting lost in the system. Grace never let me forget it, either. I stayed with her until I was seventeen. My mother died about that time. Grace took it hard. Go figure. After that, I came back from time to time to check on her. I owed her that much. She never said thank you, not once, never said a single nice thing to me. I learned not to expect it."

Meredith didn't think she would have liked Sky's family. At least she was beginning to understand a few things about Skyler Buchanan. Never expecting anything from anybody made distancing himself from others easier. "What's going to happen to the house?" she asked.

Sky didn't answer.

Meredith figured it out on her own. "Grace left it to you, didn't she?"

Sky sputtered. "I'm going to sell it. I thought I was finally finished with her. Good riddance. I was finally free. And now this. She never did a damn nice thing for me when she was alive. Why did she do something nice after she died?"

Meredith thought the real question was why couldn't she have done something nice sooner? It was high time somebody was nice to this man. Since she was in love with him, it looked as if that someone was going to be her.

She felt him looking at her, staring, really. Finally, he said, "Did you really follow me all the way to Box Elder because you thought I had a mistress and eight or nine kids?"

"Actually, I was thinking more along the lines of five or six." She smiled. When he did, too, something turned over in her chest. "I know how it feels to survive a crummy childhood, Sky. About this gene pool you mentioned. Should I see a specialist now? I mean, hunchbacks, fangs and horned monsters don't run in your family, do they?"

"Not all monsters look like monsters on the outside."

"This baby isn't going to be a monster inside or out. You're a good, decent man. If you didn't learn those qualities from your family, perhaps they're inherent in your personality. That's good. I'm even more convinced that this child is going to be delightful."

He didn't seem to know how to respond to that. After

floundering around for a few seconds, he said, "I asked you to marry me. You turned me down. If that kid really is mine, I don't see what else I can do."

If. She couldn't ignore that little word before, and she couldn't ignore it now. "I didn't turn you down, Sky."

"Sure you did."

"I said I don't know you well enough to marry you."

He took his time rising to his feet. Standing on the cracked sidewalk at the base of the steps, he said, "I don't have my pocket translator handy. That sounded like no to me."

She smiled despite his condescending manner. "That wasn't my intention."

"Are you saying you will marry me?" he asked.

"Not exactly."

He stared at her long and hard, his green eyes steady deep in the shadow of his Stetson. "What, exactly?"

"I'm saying I might."

"You might."

She smiled again. She couldn't help it. It just felt so nice not to be the one parroting for a change. "Yes. That is, I might."

Suddenly, the sun beating down on Sky's back felt unbearably hot. Meredith was sitting in the same sun, and yet she appeared comfortable and completely at ease. Her green slacks still had their crease. The matching top with its embroidered trim looked as pretty as a picture. He was becoming accustomed to the unusual combination of eyes so brown and hair so blond. He was even becoming accustomed to the zing that went through him every time he got within touching distance of her. He could think of worse fates than marrying her, and crawling into bed next to her every night.

"When *might* you marry me?" he asked.

Her eyes, artful and serene, crinkled at the corners as she pondered that. "I'm not sure," she answered. "But I think I'll know when the time is right."

The zing moved over, making room for confusion and a small dose of irritation. "Help me out here, Meredith. To me, that sounded suspiciously like that's for you to know and me to find out."

She rose blithely to her feet, the movement bringing her within a few feet of him. This close, he could smell the scent of her shampoo, could see the dark ring around her irises. "Don't worry, Sky," she said, her voice a husky murmur, letting him know that she was aware of the attraction, too. "I promise you'll be the first to know."

"What do we do in the meantime?" His gaze strayed to her mouth, a serious mistake for a man who was holding on to his control by a thread.

"In the meantime, I'd like to get to know you better."

A knot rose in Sky's throat. Other than a few of his teachers in grade school, an old man who'd taken Sky under his wing one summer and taught him how to rope and ride, and Jake McKenna, nobody had ever made much of an effort to get to know him better.

"How do you propose to do that?" he asked quietly. Actually, he had a few suggestions.

"Why don't you come to my house for dinner on Saturday?"

Dinner wasn't one of them. "We call it supper out here. Saturday?" he asked.

"Yes, at seven. Would Sunday work better for you?"

"You want to cook for me?"

"Unless you'd rather cook for me."

He held up both hands the way he might to stop a Mack truck. "Other than grilled cheese and toast, my only specialties are three siren chili and eggs." The green tinge creeping over her features reminded him that she nauseated easily these days. "Why don't we go out to supper? That way you won't have to overdo."

Several moments of silence followed. She seemed to be considering his invitation. In the end, she placed a hand over her stomach, as if to calm it. "I'd love to share a meal with you, Sky." Although her voice trailed away, Sky heard the 'but' before she said it out loud. "But I think it would be best to keep things private, just between you and me, for the time being."

Something about that bothered the back of his mind. While he was mulling it over, she said, "Trust me." As if she knew that was asking a lot, she told him goodbye then left.

He stayed in the hot midday sun long after she drove away. She'd followed him to Box Elder. He still couldn't believe she'd done that. No one else ever had. Maybe she really wasn't like the other women he knew. Maybe she especially wasn't like his mother and grandmother. Maybe her word meant something.

Maybe.

Then again, maybe not.

Sky sat on the edge of his tailgate, his legs stretched out straight, the heels of his cowboy boots resting on the ground. Other than an occasional swat at a buzzing insect, he remained perfectly still.

Meredith had promised not to overdo. She hadn't overdone. She wasn't even home. Trust me, she'd said.

Yeah, right.

They'd agreed on seven o'clock. He'd arrived at six-thirty. Criminy, he'd been ready at six. Now it was going on eight. He was half-starved, and completely agitated.

The diner closed at seven on Saturdays. Which meant that it was too late to go there to eat.

Sky jerked to his feet. It was possible he slammed the tailgate closed with more force than was necessary. It was also possible that Meredith had noticed, since she pulled into the alley and parked next to him about the same time he strode to the truck's door and gave it a good yank.

"Sky!" She popped out of her car with seemingly little effort. "What are you doing here?"

"What do you mean what am I doing here? It's eight o'clock. You said seven."

Her eyebrows drew together. "Yes, I did, but I was expecting you at seven tomorrow."

He did a double take. "I was sure we agreed on Saturday."

"And then I mentioned Sunday. Oh, dear. I guess we didn't leave things real clear, did we?"

That was it. No faultfinding, no reproach, just a simple sharing of responsibility and a calm acceptance that could only be taken at face value. Sky didn't see any reason to grin like an idiot. Luckily, she reached onto the passenger seat for a white paper sack, and didn't see. By the time she straightened, he had his expression under control. "Where have you been, anyway?" he asked.

"I saw an ad in the newspaper for an estate sale down in Murdo. I didn't find any good antiques, but a vender was selling these huge roast beef sandwiches. It's too much for me. Would you like half?" She handed him half of the wrapper without waiting for him to answer. "As long as we're both here, I guess tonight's as good a night as any to get started. What's your favorite color?"

The next thing Sky knew, he'd taken a bite of the thickest, juiciest, most tender roast beef sandwich he'd ever tasted, and had said, "Blue, I guess."

"Mine's green. What was your favorite subject in school? No wait. It was probably whatever Miss Larsen taught, right?"

His gaze had wandered to her lips, down her neck, to her chest. Which probably explained why he answered by rote. "Actually, it was math."

"Mine was art. What's your middle name?"

"Chance."

"Chance, really? What's your favorite TV show?"

"I don't know. I don't own a working television. What are you doing, Meredith?"

"I'm trying to get to know you better. It might be easier if you didn't stare at my breasts the entire time we talk."

Easier for her, maybe, he thought. A tall order for him. He gave it his best shot. They ate standing up, Sky leaning against his truck, Meredith against her car four or five feet away. They discussed the weather, the so-called decline in family values, politics and religion, all the topics the experts claimed were taboo early in a relationship. The thought gave him pause. Was that what they were having? A relationship?

Shadows stretched across the entire width of the alley by the time they ran out of things to talk about. A moth fluttered against the bare bulb over her back door. Somewhere, a dog barked. And something scuttled in the bushes nearby. "It's getting late, Sky."

Sky could have done with another sandwich, and another entire evening spent talking to Meredith. Better yet, he could have spent an entire evening not talking to Meredith. His gaze homed in on her mouth, and a few of the things he wouldn't have minded doing when he wasn't talking filtered into his mind with amazing clarity. He eased closer. "It isn't that late, Meredith."

"Maybe not for you, but I turn in early these days. I'm

not kidding. I set the timer on the television, and ten minutes later, I'm out like a light.''

"I don't have a television, remember?" He shifted a shoulder, the action bringing him closer still.

"Sky."

"Hmm?"

Meredith's eyes closed slightly, and she breathed through her mouth. "You'd better stop right there."

But he didn't stop. He was going to kiss her. Meredith wanted it, almost as much as she wanted her next breath. She took her next breath, but not the kiss. Turning her head at the last second, she said, "I know what you need." One of his eyebrows rose knowingly. She would have smiled, but she didn't trust herself to stop with just a smile, so she twirled around and called, "I'll be right back."

She unlocked the back door. Flipping lights on as she went, she hurried into a back room she used for storage, thinking that had been a close one. She'd given her relationship with Sky a great deal of thought. Every day she became more convinced that he was worth the risk to her heart. Somehow, she had to prove to him that she was worth the risk to his. That was going to take time. Time was one thing she had a lot of these days. Spying the item she was looking for, she hoisted it into her arms, and retraced her footsteps.

"What's that?" Sky asked when she returned.

"Trust me, it's not a bomb." Meredith knew precisely which word had altered his expression. "It's a television, silly. Consider it a gift. Now you'll have something to do when you go to bed tonight. And the next time I ask you about your favorite show, you'll have no excuses." She heaved the small, used set toward him, leaving him little choice but to take it. "Goodnight, Sky."

He eased away, walking backwards toward his truck.

Meredith slipped through her back door, an old saying playing through her mind. 'The way to a man's heart is through his stomach.' The way to Sky's heart was much more complicated than that.

Turning out the lights in the store, she went upstairs. She'd left the windows open, and had expected to hear Sky's truck start and drive away. Instead, voices carried on the quiet air. One was Sky's. The other was sultry and deep and very, very feminine.

"I do declare, Skyler. You gave me a fright."

Sky finished sliding the television onto the passenger seat before glancing at the woman who'd spoken. "Sorry about that Pamela Sue."

"You're such a gentleman, Skyler. How could a girl help but forgive you?" She spoke in that sensual murmur she used on most of the single men and a good percentage of the married ones as well. "What are y'all doing back here, anyway?"

Still feeling the aftereffects of being near Meredith, Sky took his time closing the passenger door. "Nothing much," he said quietly.

The next time he looked, Pamela Sue had strolled closer. A little too close for propriety or comfort. "What are you doing, Pamela Sue?"

"I was just takin' a little old walk all by my lonesome."

"Where's Grover?"

"He's visiting his mother. He visits her every night. Every night, Skyler. Don't you find that just a tad bit peculiar?" She wet her lips and heaved her chest, giving renewed meaning to the term heaving bosoms.

Pamela Sue had answered the ad and moved to Jasper Gulch a few years ago. It hadn't taken her long to land a husband. It hadn't taken her long to get bored with married life, either. Sure Grover was the world's biggest pansy. But vows were vows.

"I mean, would you visit your mother every night if you had a woman like me at home? You don't have to answer that, sugar. I know what a man like you would do."

Whoa. Sky's backward step brought his back flush with his truck.

"Did you know the door leading to the apartment over the clothing store is unlocked?"

Sky cleared his throat. "Look, Pamela Sue…"

She laid a hand on his arm and squeezed in a very provocative way. "Don't you ever long for fun and excitement, Skyler? I wouldn't tell anybody. It could be our little secret. I know you're a free spirit, and I wouldn't dream of trying to change y'all. You could think of it as a gift, with no strings."

Pamela Sue was like a lot of women. In her mid-thirties, she was pretty enough, even with her big, bleached blond hair and painted lips and fingernails. She sure as shootin' had all the right parts in all the right places. But no matter what she said about no strings, a man was sure to get tangled up real good in a gift like the one she was offering.

"I've got to be up early tomorrow. The boys and I are moving the herd to the stretch of land spanning Sugar Creek."

"You sure?" she pouted.

"Yeah."

"Aw, shucks." She wet her lips again, and heaved her chest all over again. "Maybe another time."

Sky couldn't think of a fitting reply that wasn't nasty or a blatant lie. Therefore, he gave his hat a little tug and started around to the other side of his truck without saying anything. Thankfully, she took the hint and disappeared through the side alley, probably to search for some other, more willing man.

Women. Ultimately, they were all alike. So were a lot of men. By the time Sky reached the driver side door, he was scowling so hard his face hurt. What were vows, really, except promises people chose to break? Vows, promises, gifts. They all came with strings that could tie a man up in knots or be cut at a moment's notice.

He found himself staring at the portable television resting on the passenger seat. His face relaxed. Maybe some gifts came without strings. Then he thought about the baby Meredith said was his. It was possible. He wasn't sure how likely it was, though.

Still scowling, he gave the key a good turn, put the truck in gear, and pulled out of the alley.

The knock on her door sounded at five minutes before seven. Meredith answered it immediately. Sure enough, Sky was standing on her doorstep, his eyes in the shadow of his Stetson, his chin darkened by a day-old beard. In his arms was the television she'd given him the previous night. "I tried every channel. Nothing was on."

She opened the door farther, and gestured him in before she did something really foolish like kiss him. He walked inside, kicking the door closed behind him. He placed the television on a stand next to the old drawer where the mother cat was busy grooming her seven kittens.

Eyeing Meredith closely, he said, "Why are you looking at me like that?"

"How am I looking at you?"

"Like this."

Meredith swallowed, blinked, floundered. Maybe next time she would know better than to ask. Maybe next time, her knees wouldn't be in danger of turning to jelly simply because he was looking at her as if he liked what he saw, as if he wanted what he saw.

Giving herself a mental shake, she started up the stairs. "Dinner's almost ready. I hope you like lasagna. Before you say anything about me going to too much trouble, I wanted to."

He removed his hat upon entering her apartment, placing it on a low table. Noticing that he moved a little more stiffly than usual, she said, "Did you get the herd moved to greener pastures?"

The innocent-sounding question caught Sky smack-dab in the middle of taking a deep breath of some of the best smelling food he'd ever sniffed. "How did you know we moved the herd today?"

She redistributed her weight to one foot, tipped her head slightly, and slanted him a smile that nearly buckled his knees. Without saying a word, she gestured to the open window. And understanding dawned.

"You heard Pamela Sue's little invitation."

"I heard your answer."

Suddenly, Sky knew how it would feel to be ten feet tall.

"Are you hungry?" she asked.

"To tell you the truth," he said, taking a step in her direction, "right this minute, I could take or leave food."

"I feel the same way, Sky." She took a backward step. When he took another forward one, she said, "And right about now, it would only take a feather to sweep me into your arms." Again, she stepped backward.

"Sweetheart, you're moving in the wrong direction."

She held up a hand. "No I'm not. I'm trying to do the right thing. The more I know you, the more I like you, and the more I like you, the more I want...what you want. That's why I'm appealing to your sensibility."

"My sensibility?"

She nodded. "We started our relationship in the wrong place the first time we met. I'm trying not to repeat the mistake."

"I'm listening, Meredith."

She pushed her hair behind her ears. Fiddling with the dainty little collar of a dynamite pantsuit the color of real butter, now that he took the time to notice, she said, "Neither of us was thinking clearly that night. We were hurting, or lonely, or sad, or whatever you want to call it. It happened, and neither of us was to blame. But we can't let it happen again."

"You're referring to sex."

Meredith's throat convulsed on a swallow. Even that first night had been more than sex to her. She'd been wondering how a woman went about convincing a man with a good heart but a wary soul that she was trustworthy. Last night, after she'd heard him in the alley with that woman named Pamela Sue, she'd realized it wasn't simply a matter of her *wanting* him to trust her. She needed him to trust her, to believe in her. It was what every honest person needed.

A timer went off in the kitchen. Slipping her hands into oven mitts, she removed the crusty rolls, lasagna, and green bean casserole. The entire time she'd been preparing a meal for him, she'd felt as if she were a child and was playing house. The only child among them was the one growing inside her. For that child's sake, she wanted more than pretend.

She closed the oven door and looked at him across the narrow expanse of her tiny kitchen. "I've been thinking a lot about our relationship."

"And?"

"I understand why you don't trust women. Maybe

someday, you'll trust me. Until then, I don't think we should tell anyone that we met before I moved here.'' When he started to object, she rushed on. "People will talk. And I don't want this child to grow up the object of hurtful gossip. Until you believe this baby is yours, it's better that nobody else knows.''

"Are you telling me that unless I say I believe you, I have to keep our relationship a secret?''

"Put that way it sounds like an ultimatum.''

"How would you put it?''

He was closing himself off again. The last time she'd mentioned it, he'd responded by kissing her senseless. She needed to keep her wits about her, so she let it go. "I don't want you to merely *say* you believe me.''

He didn't jump in proclaiming that he did indeed believe her. Oh, no, he remained perfectly still. He was nothing if not honest. She was honest, too. Attraction had brought them together. That attraction had led to an act that had led to this baby. She wanted a relationship, a lasting relationship, with her child's father. That required more than attraction. It required trust and respect. And love. If any one of those ingredients was missing, the relationship was doomed to fail. Now, how could she make Sky see that?

"Sometimes people do the right thing for the wrong reasons, Sky. Sometimes they do the wrong thing for the right reasons. I'm trying to do the right thing for the right reason.''

"You mean for the baby.''

For the baby, she thought, and for Sky, and her, too.

"You want to pretend that this powerful force of nature that's between us doesn't exist?'' he asked.

"No. I just don't think we should tell anyone else that it exists.''

He didn't reply for a long time. When he did, his voice

was a dull monotone. "If that's what you want, I'll keep it to myself."

She released the breath she'd been holding.

"What do we do in the meantime?" he asked.

In the meantime, she was going to go on believing in him, being honest with him, and kind to him. One day, she hoped he would have as much blind faith in her.

"In the meantime," she said, glancing at the table she'd set earlier, "let's eat."

Chapter Nine

"Norbert and Ned came into the store today. Would you grab that sweet red pepper, Sky? And while you're in the fridge, I could use that cucumber and cheese, too."

Sky unfolded his arms and uncrossed his ankles, then opened the refrigerator door. He didn't have to move far. Meredith's kitchen could practically fit in his back pocket.

"What did Ned and Norbert have to say?" Depositing the items she'd requested on the counter next to the sink, he returned to his former position near the stove, right down to the crossed ankles and folded arms.

"Neil's trying to find somebody to take over for him at the feed store, for one thing. Ned and Norbert are looking for someone to run the ranch. And evidently some firm down in Nashville wants to work on their image. For a fee of course. And they discarded the names The Triple A's, The Jasper Gents, and The Anderson Brothers, and are going with Dakota."

Sky made one of those affirmative sounds men made without opening their mouths. He didn't mention that he already knew about the musical group's name. He had better things to do. Meredith was putting the finishing touches on supper, or dinner as she called it. Sky was watching.

She went from the sink to the cutting board, to the cabinet, and back again. She was light on her feet, moving with an economy of motion that was the next thing to floating. He figured that would change one of these days.

This was the fourth Sunday in a row he'd come to her house for supper. He looked forward to it more than he cared to admit. Last week he'd arrived to the screech of her smoke alarm and smoke billowing out of the window over the alley. He'd bolted up the stairs only to find her apartment okay but supper reduced to charred rubble. They'd eaten peanut butter and jelly sandwiches. Sky had never been much of a peanut butter and jelly man. So it wasn't the food that drew him.

"Somebody," she said, drying her hands on a yellow kitchen towel, "in this town," she dropped the towel and picked up the bowl of fresh salad, "is very good," she handed the salad to him, and finally met his gaze, "at coming up with the most appropriate and fitting names. Congratulations. You've done it again."

He didn't know how she knew Dakota had been his suggestion. He only knew that when she smiled, a zing went through him. And he wanted to chuck supper, and drag her off to bed. The wanting was nothing new. But his feelings for her were. They were deepening, and that just plain hadn't happened to him before.

"Maybe they'll dedicate their first album to you," she said, placing the casserole in the center of her small kitchen table.

Sky figured it was more likely that they would dedicate it to Meredith. She had that effect on people.

They sat down. They even bowed their heads, when Sky

had never prayed before a meal in his life until he knew her. And then they ate. They talked easily, and laughed often. When they were finished, he helped with the dishes, and they laughed and talked some more.

The phone in the living room rang just as she was letting the water out of the sink. While Sky finished drying, he couldn't help overhearing her end of the conversation. From the little she said, he deduced she was talking to a man. She didn't mention a name, but whoever it was wanted to see her. She was smooth, Sky would give her that, for she turned down the invitation to attend the Anderson Brothers' going away party next month, suggesting a friendly daytime chat over lunch, instead.

She hung up the phone, returning to the kitchen as if nothing out of the ordinary had occurred. "Where were we?" she asked. "Oh, I remember. The kittens are six weeks old, and Sharla is taking it upon herself to find suitable homes for them. You should hear her interview the prospective pet owners."

Sky placed the last dry dish on the counter before looking at her. He hadn't seen this particular pale green dress before. It was loose fitting, simple in style. Lovely. "Does that happen often?" he asked.

She stretched on tiptoe to place a dish on a high shelf, the action drawing the fabric tight to her body, conforming to the curve of her breast. Closing the cabinet, she crossed her arms, and ducked her head, the sudden movement drawing his gaze back to her face. Judging by her knowing expression, it had been an intentional move on her part. "Do I often receive requests for dates, you mean?"

He nodded. She always seemed to know what his questions referred to. He wondered how she did that.

"Oh, I get one or two requests a week. The men of Jasper Gulch are just being friendly."

"If you'd tell them the baby's mine, they'd stop asking for dates."

Meredith held perfectly still. Sky was clean-shaven tonight, and he'd gotten his hair cut since the last time she saw him. He was a handsome rogue in shaggy hair and whiskers. Spit and polished, he took her breath away. Still, as far as she was concerned, the way he'd just clamped his mouth shut was very telling. "Do you believe the baby is yours, Sky?"

He held her gaze for several seconds, but didn't reply. Talk about actions speaking louder than words.

She changed the subject, and assured herself she wasn't hurt. He still didn't believe, beyond the shadow of a doubt, that the baby was his. She hadn't expected this to be easy. They still had plenty of time. Nearly five months, to be exact.

As she had the three previous Sundays, she poured them each a glass of lemonade, then led the way into her little living room. Turning on the television, she settled on one end of the sofa, Sky in the adjacent chair, and they watched a program about angels, her favorite, and since it was the only show Sky watched, it was his favorite, too.

"Evenin' ladies. What'll it be?" Boomer Brown asked in a booming baritone befitting his name.

Crystal Galloway and Meredith sidled up next to the bar. Using a perfect French accent, Crystal said, "Your finest French Bordeaux, monsieur."

Since Crystal was fluent in several languages, no one ever knew which accent she would use when she visited the Crazy Horse. But the results were always the same. Either Boomer or his wife, DoraLee took a bottle of chilled grape juice from the refrigerator below the bar and poured a generous portion into one of the two inexpensive fluted glasses DoraLee had picked up for a song at the dime store's going-out-of-business sale last year.

As long as he had the refrigerator door open tonight, Boomer reached for the carton of milk. "Don't get too rowdy now," he said, sliding a tall glass of milk toward Meredith.

"We'll try to keep it down," Meredith replied.

Taking a sip of milk, she surveyed the room. There was so much noise and commotion she couldn't tell which song was playing on the jukebox. Four old-timers were involved in an intense game of poker at a table in the corner. "How was the picture show?" that sweet old Cletus McCully called after he'd raked in a stack of chips and somebody's pocket watch.

"It was good," Meredith said.

"But predictable," Crystal added.

The Crazy Horse was crowded. The Anderson Brothers had spent a lot of evenings here, and all the regulars had come to say goodbye. The mechanical bull was charged up tonight. Several cowboys and ranchers stood in a semi-circle around the contraption by the big double doors way in the back. They sure were raising a ruckus. Meredith was more interested in the man watching her quietly from a table nearby. Her heart rate climbed and her breathing deepened, just as it did every time she got lost in the expression deep in Sky's green eyes.

"How's it going, Meredith?" one of the local boys asked as she passed.

"You're lookin' good tonight, Meredith," another spouted.

"Fine, Forrest. You don't look so bad yourself, Butch."

"Then why won'choo marry me?" Butch slurred.

Forrest admonished his drunken friend. "There's about

as good a chance that she'll marry you as there is that she'll name the kid after me.''

Meredith winked at Forrest, who raised his beer bottle to her in a silent toast. A woman at a nearby table said, ''Do you have any names picked out, Meredith?''

Smiling at the sheriff's wife, Meredith said, ''I have a few ideas, but all I know for sure is that if it's a girl, I won't name her Grace or Lauralee.''

Crystal took the seat that was miraculously vacant as well as pushed out next to Sky, who apparently was choking on a pretzel. Meredith slid onto the chair next to Crystal. Crystal struck up a conversation with Ned Anderson; Meredith's gaze met Sky's. His face was still slightly red from his little choking spell, but he smiled at her and she at him. She read the want in his eyes. Before anyone else saw, they both looked elsewhere.

All in all, she thought things were going quite well. The weeks had fallen into a routine. She picked Logan and Olivia up from school every Tuesday. And she and Crystal took in a movie most Saturdays. Business wasn't bad, either. She'd finished reupholstering Cletus McCully's sofa. Two eccentric women who'd reportedly won the lottery before moving to Jasper Gulch a few years ago had purchased several of her finest antiques. Last week Meredith had hosted a seminar on painting, sponging, ragging and marbling techniques. Sharla was proving to be quite an asset. While many of the girls she'd graduated with had gone away to college or moved to the city, Sharla had agreed to stay on at Hidden Treasures. Of course, that might have had something to do with Billy Schmidt. Holly was a gem, too. Although she still didn't smile a lot, she came in every day after school and on alternating Saturdays. Meredith had a friendly lunch with the shy but willing men of Jasper Gulch from time to time, and every

Sunday, Sky came to dinner, or supper as he called it. He was an intriguing man. In public, he was on his best behavior. In private was another thing. He always said please and thank you, and helped with the dishes. More often than not, he kissed her senseless before he left. They rarely talked about the baby. Sometimes, she caught him looking at her stomach, and she knew he was thinking, wondering, questioning. He wasn't ready to believe beyond a shadow of a doubt, that the baby was his. Sometimes, she worried that he never would.

She reminded herself that he'd grown up without a woman's touch, with few acts of kindness, and very little honesty. It was a shame, but it wasn't too late. She was only five months along. There was still plenty of time.

Meredith took a sip of her hot cocoa. On the other side of the table, Holly warmed her hands around her cup; Sharla's and Crystal's were already half gone. They'd come to the diner to celebrate the beginning of the festive season. Fat, wet snowflakes drifted to the ground outside, gathering on windowsills, sticking to the newly decorated lampposts lining Main Street. The hot chocolate was good; the scenery was lovely. The only problem Meredith could see was the nine gray-haired women talking heatedly on the other side of the room.

"Pregnant! Can you believe it?" Harriet Andrews said in a whisper sharp enough to penetrate steel. "And Pamela Sue swears it's my poor boy's child."

"How is that sweet Grover doing, anyway?" Edith Ferguson, the current president of the Ladies Aid Society asked in a whisper even louder than Harriet's.

"You know my boy. He puts on a brave face, but inside, his heart's breaking."

Meredith, Crystal, Sharla and Holly exchanged similar

looks. Crystal, whose back was to the group of women sitting in their usual spot in front of the window, rolled her eyes and whispered, "Grover Andrews, brave? Just once I'd like someone to remind Harriet that her boy is over forty years old."

"Brandy!" Edith Ferguson practically shrieked.

Meredith, Crystal, Holly and Sharla all jumped.

"Keep that coffee coming, dear," the other woman called when the waitress poked her head out of the kitchen. "This emergency meeting will more than likely take a while."

"Emergency meeting, my eye," Crystal said under her breath. "Have any of you heard them say a word about anything except Pamela Sue's little bombshell?"

Meredith shook her head. Actually, she hadn't heard anybody talk about much of anything else ever since the rumor had leaked yesterday morning. Her gaze followed Brandy Schafer's progress as she refilled one cup after another, but in her mind, Meredith couldn't seem to stop envisioning how Pamela Sue had propositioned Sky three months ago. He'd turned her down. People were saying somebody other than Grover hadn't.

"Why, that little hussy might have gotten her claws into my boy, but I knew it was only a matter of time and he'd be moving back home where he belongs. Such a good boy, my Grover. I don't know what he ever saw in that, that…well, suffice it to say I don't know what he ever saw in Pamela Sue."

"I thought they were in love," Brandy said, refilling the coffee cup nearest her.

Edith made a disparaging sound. "He fell in love with the fit of her sweater." Harriet gasped, and Edith added, "He is a man, Harriet."

"But what if the baby's his?" Brandy asked, moving on to the next cup.

In the ensuing silence that fell over the far table, Crystal whispered, "Ten, nine, eight, seven…"

As if realizing her mistake, Brandy, who was a hopeless romantic, said, "I mean, they're married, right? Wouldn't it be better if the baby was his?"

"Six, five, four…"

Harriet fanned herself as if she might faint.

"Better for who?" one of the other members quipped.

"Three, two…"

"Why, for Grover, and Pamela Sue."

"Merciful heavens!"

The coffee carafe shook in Brandy's right hand. "All right, then, for the baby."

"One," Holly, Sharla and Crystal whispered together.

"That baby is not my Grover's!"

Crystal mimed an explosion sound. "There goes Brandy's tip."

Sharla giggled behind her hand. "I worked here last summer. Believe me, the Ladies Aid Society never tips. Look, at the time. I have to go home. Billy's picking me up at five. Thanks for the hot chocolate, Meredith. Decorating the tree in the store was fun, wasn't it, Holly?"

Holly nodded. "Especially since Dad doesn't want to put up a tree this year."

"It must be rough. They say the first year is the hardest," Sharla said. "Do you need a ride home?"

Holly shook her head. "My dad's picking me up at two."

After Sharla bustled off, Meredith, Crystal and Holly sipped their cocoa in silence. When hers was finished, Holly said, "Do you think that's true? About the first year being the hardest, I mean."

Meredith was still trying to come up with an appropriate response when Crystal said, "I don't know many living people who stay in sackcloth and ashes forever."

Holly pondered that for the few moments before her father pulled up outside. Watching her walk away, Meredith said, "You have a knack for knowing what to say and how to say it."

"This is the first time I've ever been accused of that. My biggest downfall in college was my people skills. One of my professors gave me an A-minus because of it."

Something told Meredith that Crystal hadn't gotten many A-minuses. "Well, you're certainly good with Holly. You'd make a wonderful mother."

Meredith had intended to launch right into her next question, but Crystal's face had darkened with an unreadable emotion. Crystal Galloway was extremely intelligent. And opinionated. Lord, what an understatement. Her hair was naturally curly, her eyes tilted slightly, giving her an exotic look. She happened to have a gorgeous face and a body that could have sold perfume or lingerie. And yet, every once in a while, a faraway expression stole across her face. She grew quiet, causing Meredith to wonder what she was thinking about. Or who. "Are you okay?" Meredith asked.

The moment passed, and Crystal nodded. "Of course. Never been better."

At the other table, the leaders of the Ladies Aid Society were all still talking about Pamela Sue. Pamela Sue's mother-in-law was talking the loudest of all.

Meredith had only spoken to Pamela Sue briefly. They had little in common, but this whole episode reminded Meredith how hurtful gossip was. Even if Pamela Sue's baby was her husband's, the people of Jasper Gulch would always wonder, would always watch for similarities to

some other man. Maybe Pamela Sue deserved it, maybe
not. But the child was innocent, and the child was the one
who was going to suffer the most. Meredith's baby could
have suffered the same fate. She'd done the right thing by
keeping Sky's paternity a secret from everyone except him.

The baby moved inside her, rolling gently from one side
to the other. Maternal love poured through Meredith. The
baby was due in two months. Placing a hand on her
rounded girth, she decided it was time to stop putting this
off. "Crystal, I have a favor to ask. You can say no if you
want to, but I was wondering…"

Crystal pushed her unruly tumble of blond hair behind
her shoulders, and said, "What do you need? A kidney?
A loan? A labor coach?"

"How did you know I needed a labor coach?"

Crystal pulled a face. "Whew. For a second there, I
thought you were going to say you really do need a kidney,
and I'm terrified of needles."

"Then you wouldn't mind attending prenatal classes
with me?"

That unreadable emotion flickered far back in Crystal's
eyes again. "I'd be honored, Meredith. Now it's my turn
to run. Let me know where and when the classes begin,
okay?" Gathering her long wool coat, gloves and hat, she
said, "Do you want to go to a movie tonight?"

"I'm watching Logan and Olivia for Wes and Jayne."

"I'll talk to you tomorrow, then." Crystal headed for
the door. She stopped at the Ladies Aid Society's table
long enough to say hello and mention Meredith's request.
Although not nearly as juicy as the Pamela Sue gossip, the
Jasper Gulch grapevine would spread this new information
from one end of the county to the other before sundown.
Sky would undoubtedly hear about it. She wondered how

he was going to feel about it. She doubted she would have to wait long to find out.

"'Livia, what are you doing?"

"I'm makin' the snowman's tummy big like Aunt Meredith's. It's a pregnant snowman."

"It is not a pregnant snowman."

"Is so."

"Uh-uh."

"Uh-huh."

Sky stood in the driveway, one hand on the door, one foot on the running board. He and Clive Hendricks had been looking over Wes's new bull when Meredith had arrived at the Stryker house. Now, she and the kids were building a snowman near the house. Wes and Jayne Stryker had already driven away, and Clive was close behind them.

This wasn't the first time he'd seen Meredith today. At a few minutes before closing time, he'd gone around to the store's back door and let himself in. She'd been on her knees in front of an overstuffed chair. She'd looked up at him as if she'd been expecting him. And she'd smiled.

She loved him.

The realization had nearly bowled him over. If she loved him, she should marry him, dammit. It occurred to him that maybe that was the problem. Maybe the reason she wouldn't marry him was because she loved him. That sounded crazy even to him. But it made sense. If she loved him, and it was starting to look as if she did, she wouldn't want to hurt him by trying to pass off somebody else's kid as his.

He'd closed the door. Without so much as a howdy-you-do, he said, "If I'm the father, and even if I'm not, I should be the one helping you through labor."

Her smile had slid away like the snow melting off the roof. This time, she hadn't said, "If, Sky?" But the question had been in her eyes.

He'd felt like something he'd stepped in.

By the time she found her feet, she'd done what she could to mask her hurt. Watching her now, Sky felt even worse. She was helping Logan and Olivia with their snowman. All of them were laughing because her stomach kept getting in the way. She was beautiful, her hair, her voice, her laughter.

Until ten minutes ago, he hadn't heard the gossip about Pamela Sue. Clive had been only too happy to relay the information, along with a lengthy rant about how he'd demand a DNA paternity test if he were Grover.

Now Sky knew that Meredith had asked Crystal because if she'd asked him, people would have talked. They would have speculated that the baby might have been his. Meredith was right. Gossip like that could only hurt a child. None of this would have happened if she would have agreed to tell people that it was his from the beginning.

She chose that moment to look his way, her gaze meeting his from the other side of the yard. She said something to Logan and Olivia. A heartbeat later, the kids waved wholeheartedly. He returned their waves and their grins, but it wasn't easy, because he wanted to vault over Logan's snow fort and kiss her. He couldn't, because those kids would see, and they would tell. So, instead of kissing her senseless, he held her gaze and strode closer. He removed his hat when he reached her. Feeling like a schoolboy shuffling from one foot to the other, he said, "Clive just told me. About Pamela Sue."

Her eyebrows lifted fractionally. A moment later, she smiled kindly, and he was forgiven. Something intense flared through him, something he'd never felt in exactly this way. It wasn't just a simple case of a man wanting a woman. There was nothing simple about any of this, and hadn't been from the start. He didn't know what it meant, or what he was going to do about it. He only knew that…

The snowball hit him with a cold, wet thud. If he'd been paying attention, he would have noticed Logan lobbing it in his direction. He dodged the one Olivia tossed. When Meredith reached down for a handful of snow, Sky did, too.

Laughter, a boy's and a girl's, and a man's and a woman's, rang out over the snowy yard. A one-eyed snowman and several horses watched the scuffle that ensued.

Meredith reveled in the joy and merriment of the moment. Sky may not have been ready to trust in her word completely, but she was pretty sure he was falling in love with her. The knowledge started a spark in her chest, radiating outward, rising like hope.

She shrieked and played, being careful not to overdo. Brushing the snow that Logan, the little traitor, had washed her face with, Meredith counted her blessings. She had Logan and Olivia. And she was pretty sure Sky was coming to love her. She had two more months to gain his trust.

And if he never did? She did her best to ignore the niggling doubt that filtered into her thoughts more and more these days. She wouldn't worry about that now. Besides, if all else failed, she still had an ace up her sleeve. Her due date was the second of February, precisely nine months after the night she'd spent with Sky. It was beginning to look as if it might come right down to the wire. That was okay. There was still time.

Chapter Ten

"How does that feel?" Meredith asked.

Sky's only answer was a sigh.

"How about this?"

"Hmm." More of the same. The only illumination in her living room came from the lights on her Christmas tree and the television that was on, as usual. Someone Sky probably should have recognized was counting the minutes before the ball dropped in Times Square.

"Ah, Meredith," he said, groaning softly as she worked a kink out of a muscle in the back of his neck, "you're killing me with kindness."

"Do you want me to stop?"

He shook his head. He never wanted her to stop.

He'd arrived late, and had left his snow-covered boots out on the stairs. His hat hung on a peg by the door, his shirt over one of her kitchen chairs. Sitting in front of Meredith, barefoot and shirtless, his eyes kept drifting closed, and his head tipped forward as she smoothed and kneaded the soreness from his tense muscles.

"You're tied up in knots," she whispered, moving down his back, one vertebra at a time.

Taking a deep, shuddering breath, he sighed again. He'd been tied up in knots a lot lately. Since he'd showered before he'd arrived, it should have been the scent of his deodorant soap he smelled. He breathed in the scent of peaches. Meredith's scent. Somehow, that scent had gotten into his bunkhouse. The last time he'd gone to the house in Box Elder, he'd noticed it there, too.

He groaned deep in his throat, rotating the shoulder she was massaging. She really was killing him with kindness. She'd put her touches on his grandmother's house. It had sold the first week it went on the market. Sky figured the couple who bought it must have liked peaches. She cooked him supper nearly every Sunday. She laughed at his jokes, listened to his concerns, argued when it suited her, stimulated him, mind and body.

"Relax," she said, pressing the heel of her hand into a particularly tight muscle below his shoulder blade.

If only it was that easy.

"What did you do today?"

"We reinforced the fenced-in area behind one of the outbuildings in preparation for the bull Jake is borrowing from Wes." Sky's hands had turned numb inside his leather gloves. Since it was too early to go to Meredith's, and he'd been too agitated to sit around at his place, he'd taken Bommer for a run. When he'd gotten back to the barn, he'd discovered that a cow was down. Since Jake, Josie and Kelsey had already left to attend a party, Sky had used the phone he'd just had installed in his place, and called Luke Carson, the local veterinarian.

"The ride on Bommer didn't help this time?" she asked.

Truth was, riding like the wind helped less and less these

days. Sky could only think of one thing that would. One thing with one woman.

He closed his eyes until the Christmas tree lights blurred. And his thoughts slowed. There must have been magic in her touch, because he was in danger of sliding off the stool.

"That's it," she whispered. "Relax."

Something incredibly soft brushed the back of one shoulder. His eyes opened, and desire uncurled deep inside him.

Had she kissed him, or had he been dreaming?

"What are you thinking?" she whispered close to his ear.

"I was thinking that I wish you would hurry up and marry me so I can do what I'm imagining doing to you right now."

He didn't know whether he leaned back, or she leaned ahead, but the next thing he knew, something moved against his lower back. Or someone.

He swiveled until he was facing her. "A smile like yours, sexy and sensuous, has no business on a woman due to have a baby in a month or so."

"One month and two days." Meredith smiled again, enjoying the depth and emotion in his eyes.

She'd had a lovely holiday. Logan and Olivia had been thrilled with their gifts. She'd been thrilled to spend part of Christmas day with them. Still, some of her favorite times had been those moments she'd spent with Sky. She'd loved watching what kindness could do to a man like him. He'd asked her to marry him on Christmas again. "Now isn't the time right?" he'd asked.

She'd shaken her head gently. "Not quite." But it was close, she thought. There was only one thing missing. It wasn't love, for her or the baby. It was almost as important, certainly as fundamental to any relationship that would last. The only thing missing was trust.

She was hoping that now that the house in Box Elder had sold, Sky would be able to put the past, complete with all its untruths and disappointments, behind him. He claimed she was killing him with kindness, but he was being just as kind to her. He badgered her about putting her feet up after lunch every day. He, a man who abhorred telephones, claiming they were nooses around the neck of society, had had one installed at the bunkhouse. He'd said it was time he entered the current century. She knew he'd done it so she could reach him if she needed him, when the time came.

Taking Sky's big, work-roughened hand in both of hers, she placed it on her swollen abdomen. The baby kicked and rolled beneath his palm and fingers. The look on Sky's face made her fall farther in love.

"You are one stubborn, contrary woman, do you know that?"

"And you once told me you're not a romantic at heart."

Their eyes were level, and they shared a smile. She knew he loved her. He loved the baby, too. He would be a wonderful father.

Sky chuckled. "The kid has quite a kick."

"I'm hoping the baby will be light on its feet like you."

He closed his eyes again. He was exhausted. It made her wonder why he wasn't sleeping at night. Beneath his hand, the baby, always more active at this time of the evening, continued to move.

Meredith had been invited to the Colters' New Year's Eve party. She was glad she'd declined. Seeing the expression on Sky's face right now had been worth the wait.

When the baby kicked particularly hard, his expression changed, growing serious, stark, painful almost, as if filled with yearning. Tears gathered in her eyes. He was hoping the baby was his. Meredith wished she knew what to say to convince him. But this was a conclusion he had to reach on his own.

The phone jangled in the living room. Neither of them moved. Neither of them wanted to break the connection that had formed where his hand rested on the child growing inside her.

The answering machine picked up on the sixth ring. "Meredith, this is DoraLee Brown over at the Crazy Horse. If you're home, would you pick up?"

She hurried into the living room, Sky close behind her. Grabbing up the receiver, Meredith said, "I'm here, DoraLee. What is it?"

"There's a man over here."

"A man?" Meredith asked.

"Yes," the voice on the other end said over the commotion in the background.

"What man?"

"He says he's Sky's father. Judging by his height and green eyes, I'd have to believe him."

"What does he want?" Meredith asked DoraLee.

"What does who want?" Sky asked Meredith.

"He wants to see Sky," DoraLee answered. "Would you tell him?"

Meredith's brain was so befuddled she didn't question how DoraLee had known Sky was here. "I'll tell him, DoraLee."

"Tell me what?" Sky asked before she'd even hung up the phone.

A sense of dread came out of nowhere, closing off her windpipe. Clearing her throat, she looked up at Sky. "There's someone to see you over at the Crazy Horse."

"Who?"

"Your father."

Meredith stood at the closed door, listening to the soft tread of Sky's footsteps on the stairs. He'd paced from one end of her apartment to the other, then grabbed his shirt, buttoning it by rote. He'd shoved his hat on his head, and his feet into his boots. And then he'd left without kissing her goodbye.

Meredith lumbered across her living room and stood at the window where she had a bird's eye view of Main Street. It had started snowing hours ago. The wind was picking up, whipping the snow against the window, swirling it into drifts in doorways and around lampposts.

Main Street was deserted, except for the lone figure of a man stepping off the curb. Sky's head was down against the onslaught of icy snow, his chin tucked into the collar of his sheepskin coat. Moving with seemingly little effort, he opened the saloon door and slipped through.

Meredith shivered, chewing on her thumbnail. Realizing what she was doing, she slid her hand into the pocket of her winter-white smock. She never bit her nails.

She was nervous. Worried sick.

Sky loved her, and he loved their child. She was certain he'd been a hairsbreadth away from saying as much. He'd been putting his past behind him ever since the night they first met. Finally, tonight, he'd been on the brink of succeeding. And then DoraLee had called to say his father had shown up.

His father, who hadn't been worth the trouble it had taken to find him, who hadn't ever been a father to his son, had never thrown him so much as a crumb of kindness, certainly no fatherly love, who hadn't so much as put a dime toward supporting Sky, had shown up in Jasper

Gulch. Sky's mother had lied. Sky's father hadn't even bothered to do that.

This man's timing stunk. He was bound to remind Sky of all his reasons to distrust men and women, particularly pregnant women.

Trying to cheer herself up, she reminded herself that if all else failed, she still had the ace up her sleeve. Not even a visit from Sky's father could erase the implications when she had this child a month from now.

She hadn't even realized she'd been chewing on her thumbnail again until she lowered her hand, placing it in the small of her aching back. She must have overdone it in the store. Rubbing the sore muscles, she wondered when Sky would return.

The ache intensified, squeezing around each side until it met in the middle of her distended abdomen. She stopped rubbing her back, and simply stood, analyzing the pain. It wasn't a knee-jerk sensation. It was…strange.

After twenty or thirty seconds, it subsided. Meredith would have dismissed it, if it hadn't started up again exactly four minutes later.

She glanced at her watch, at the street below where she'd last seen Sky, and at her stomach. The baby had grown very still.

Could this be labor? Impossible. It was a month early, a month and two days. Maybe it was false labor. Please, let it be false labor. Please, please, please, please, please.

The third pain lasted longer than the first two had. A few seconds after it ended, the ball dropped in Times Square, along with the ace up her sleeve.

A hush fell over the saloon the instant Sky set foot inside. The area cowboys stared right at him when he entered. Sky nodded at Boomer, who was washing glasses behind the bar.

"Happy New Year," Boomer said, tilting his head just enough to let Sky know which direction to turn.

"Thanks, Boomer. The same to you."

"Care for a beer?"

Sky shook his head. He didn't plan to stay long enough to drink a beer.

The Crazy Horse crowd was typical for New Year's Eve. Pretty sparse, all things considered. Cletus McCully was there with a few of his cronies. The Wilkie brothers were holding up their usual end of the bar. Grover Andrews was a new face, but the handful of others weren't.

Since DoraLee had strung lights over the mechanical bull, it was out of operation. The jukebox was up and running, though. Unfortunately, it wasn't loud enough to cover the voice of the man Sky hadn't seen in nearly twenty years. "Didn't I tell you he's the spittin' image of me?"

Clive Hendricks and Keith Gurski raised their shot glasses to their mouths. "He sure is."

Sky cast Keith and Clive bland looks. He'd never had a lot of use for either of them. Leave it to them to share a table with his old man. Evidently like recognized like.

Keeping his expression under strict control, he finally looked Hank Nichols in the eye. The fact that Hank's eyes were almost identical to the eyes Sky looked at in the mirror every morning turned his stomach. "What are you doing here?"

"Can't a man visit his son around the holidays?"

Evidently, he could. He just never had.

"The boys here have been filling me in on what you've been up to." Hank pushed a chair out with his right foot.

Sky remained standing. "I can't stay."

"That's right. I heard you have a little woman."

Sky glanced at the other two men. They both shrugged. Until a few minutes ago, Sky hadn't been aware that the people of Jasper Gulch knew about him and Meredith. DoraLee *had* known where to find him tonight. He wondered why rumors had never circled back to him.

"What are you doing here, Hank?"

Hank Nichols was a few inches taller than Sky's six feet. His hair had some gray in it, his face some wrinkles. There was a good chance Sky would look a lot like him in twenty or thirty years. At least on the outside. But Sky's eyes would never lack warmth, and he would never try to pass that curl of lip off as a smile.

"What do you want, Hank?"

"I came to offer my condolences."

Sky didn't follow. "For what?"

"I heard Grace passed on."

Sky was beginning to understand. "You heard that, did you?"

Hank reached for a pretzel, pretending to study it. "Met a fella who knew somebody who lives in Box Elder. It's a small world."

Clive and Keith would have nodded, if Sky hadn't shot them a withering glare before returning his attention to Hank. "Grace died eight months ago."

"That's what her neighbor said." He turned the pretzel over, then looked up at Sky. "I decided to pay my respects. It was the least I could do."

Sky refrained from saying, "How big of you."

Hank said, "The house looked good. Real good. The neighbors said she left it to you."

Sky shrugged. And waited.

"Must have brought a pretty penny."

Even a drunken fool would have known what was coming next. As if to prove his point, both Clive and Keith shifted uncomfortably in their chairs. Of course, Hank failed to notice. He was too intent upon playing out his little charade. Reaching for his long neck bottle, he said, "I'd offer to buy you a drink, son, but I'm afraid I'm a little down on my luck."

"Imagine that."

"It isn't my fault. The woman I was living with kicked me out. You know how women can be. And I got to thinking. I hadn't seen my boy in a long time. And then that fella mentioned that old Grace finally kicked the bucket. I sure could use a little cash right now."

The jukebox changed songs, giving Sky an idea. Keeping all expression from his face, he reached into his front pocket. Not that Hank would have noticed his expression. His gaze was trained on Sky's hand.

Sky removed a few folded bills. But he dug deeper. Taking a coin between his thumb and forefinger, he held it up, then tossed the quarter to Hank. "Call someone who cares."

Chuckles and snickers broke out throughout the bar. Hank looked all around. Realizing that he was going to get no money and even less sympathy from the patrons of the bar, he rose to his feet. "I just had a flash from the past. You're just like your old lady and that old battle-ax, Grace Miller."

"You're wrong," Sky said. "I'm not like any of you. Thank God for that."

Hank smirked at the local boys. Sputtering about redneck cowboys, he left.

Boomer grinned at Sky from the other side of the bar. Forrest Wilkie proposed a toast. Cletus McCully ambled over on bowed legs. Grumbling about joints that got stiffer every year, he plunked a bottle of whiskey on the table then took a seat. "Thought maybe you could use a drink, boy," he said, a thumb hooked through his suspenders.

"No thanks, Cletus. But you go ahead."

Cletus poured himself a shot, knocked it back, then stared at Sky through faded, watery eyes. Feeling like a germ under a microscope, Sky took a seat opposite the old man. "I had no idea folks knew I was spending time with Meredith."

"Not much gets around the local grapevine."

"What are they saying?"

Cletus shrugged. "Mostly, they're wonderin' why you haven't slapped a ring on that gal's finger."

"Believe me, I've tried."

"Then you love her."

Sky scowled. "Of course I love her."

Cletus poured another shot. This time, he left it on the table. "No sense even askin' if she loves you. I've seen the way she looks at you when you ain't lookin'. I wonder why she won't marry you, then."

Sky leaned ahead, elbows on the table, his voice so low only Cletus could hear. "She says she won't marry me until I believe the baby's mine."

"Is it?"

"It would be nice, but the bottom line is it doesn't matter to me. That's the kicker. I don't need to have been the man who planted the seed. It's enough that I love her, and she loves me. Loving the kid's a given."

"Maybe this isn't about what you need."

Sky opened his mouth to argue. Nothing came out.

He glanced around him, and caught everybody looking. He would undoubtedly be the talk of the town by morning. He didn't have it in him to mind.

"Cletus?" he said, a strange thought occurring to him. "The people in this town love nothing better than gossip.

If everybody knows about Meredith and me, why haven't they shredded her reputation?''

Cletus McCully had a craggy face, and a heart big enough to take his grandson and granddaughter in after the tragic drowning accident that claimed his son and daughter-in-law's lives twenty-five years ago. He cheated at cards, but not at life. Looking Sky in the eye, he said, "What's to shred?" Sky was digesting the question when Cletus continued. "You need fuel to have a fire, boy. Have you ever known Meredith to say an unkind word about anybody? Has she ever failed to so something she said she would do? Look how she's been with Logan and Olivia. Why, a more selfish person might have tried to take them away from Wes and Jayne. Meredith said she didn't want to disrupt their lives after all they've already been through, and she hasn't. She only wanted the chance to be close to them, and that's what she's done. You know she recovered my couch? Didn't charge me a penny more than she said she would, either. Some people are as good as their word.''

The sleigh bells hanging on the back of the door jingled when Jason Tucker came in. "Brrr," he exclaimed, stomping the snow off his boots and shaking it off his hat. "Mighty strange time for a parade."

"What do you mean?" Boomer asked, sliding a beer across the bar.

"I met a procession ten minutes ago."

Everybody in the bar listened up.

"What kind of procession?" Boomer asked.

"Six cars in all, emergency lights going. Sheriff Colter was in the lead, his sirens wailing and red and blue lights flashing. At first I thought he was transporting a criminal. Remember the time that ex-con, Kipp Dawson, showed up in town? Well, it wasn't a criminal this time. The light was on in the back seat." Jason looked directly at Sky. "Why do you suppose Meredith was going toward Pierre this time of the night?"

"Meredith was in the cruiser?" Sky had jumped to his feet.

Jason nodded. "Her and Crystal Galloway and Doc Kincaid, all three. Luke and Clayt Carson's vehicles were in the procession, too. So was Wes Stryker's. Hey, where's Sky going?"

By the time Cletus said, "I believe he's on his way to the hospital in Pierre," Sky was out the door, across the street, and halfway to his truck parked in the alley behind Meredith's store.

The hospital was twenty-five miles away and the snow-covered roads were treacherous. Sky drove the entire way clutching the steering wheel with both hands, his face close to the windshield. Any good Meredith's massage had done was long gone by the time he reached the parking lot. He parked next to the vehicles from Jasper Gulch, turned off the engine and ran inside.

A dozen familiar faces turned toward him the instant he entered the waiting room. "Has she…"

Everybody started talking at once. Melody Carson remedied the problem by placing two fingers in her mouth and whistling.

"Crystal's with her," Brittany Colter said when things quieted down some.

"And Burke," Doc Kinaid's wife added.

Sky rushed to the nurse's desk. He waited three seconds for the woman to get off the phone. Since it was apparent to him that she was talking to a friend, he reached over the counter and broke the connection. "A woman just came in. She's having a baby."

"Have a seat," the nurse said, a pinched expression on her face.

"I don't want a seat. I want to know how Meredith is." Spying a sign on the wall that pointed to the maternity unit, he said, "Never mind."

"Sir. You can't..."

But he already had.

A middle-aged nurse that could have made her living playing football if she ever wanted to make a career change hung up a phone and promptly blocked his path.

"Meredith Warner," he said. "How is she?"

"She's fine. They just took her to delivery."

"Where's that?"

Just then, a nurse bustled through a set of double doors, and Sky heard a whimper that turned his stomach. Meredith.

He started in that direction. "Sir," the nurse exclaimed, chasing after him. "You can't go in there."

"Watch me." He stared at an orderly who appeared out of nowhere, his expression clearly stating, stay out of my way.

"Anybody passing this point has to wear a scrub suit."

Meredith's whimper came again. This time, he could make out Doc Kincaid's voice, too. Grabbing a scrub suit off the pile, Sky slid his arms through the holes and pushed through the double doors.

Two nurses immediately tried to block his path. "Who are you?" the first one said shrilly.

"I'm the father!"

Sky was only marginally aware of an antiseptic smell, of bright lights and stainless steel. His gaze rested on Meredith. She looked pale, scared, in pain, and yet for reasons he couldn't fathom, glad to see him.

"Sky?" Meredith's voice quavered.

He was at her side in a flash, smoothing her hair off her forehead, wanting to do more. "What is it?" he whispered.

She moistened her lips, swallowed, and tried to smile. "Now, I'll marry you."

Sky's eyes glazed over, his throat constricted.

"Uh, folks," Burke Kincaid said from the other end of the table. "Do you think you could wait a few minutes until after your baby is born?"

The room, all at once, was very quiet. But not for long.

Chapter Eleven

Sky paused in the doorway of room 212. Meredith was resting. Her eyes were closed, but he didn't think she was sleeping. Unless she'd figured out how to smile in her sleep. It wouldn't have surprised him. She was the most incredible woman he'd ever met.

The baby in her arms made a mewling sound. Meredith opened her eyes, and met Sky's gaze. He managed to hold on to the teddy bear tucked under one arm, and the roses gripped tightly in one hand, but just barely. Walking closer, his heart swelled with so much feeling he was pretty sure it had floated up to the ceiling with the balloons he'd just released. "How are you feeling?"

"Glorious." She looked down at the baby, and motioned for Sky to come closer. "We have a lot to talk about," she whispered.

Sky removed his hat, placing it on the windowsill along with the bouquet of flowers. He tucked the teddy bear at the foot of the bed then eased around to the side. He couldn't seem to take his eyes off the baby, so tiny, so perfect. "Did you want to talk about the wedding?" he whispered.

"That, and a name befitting Skyler Buchanan's son."

He simply couldn't believe what hearing those words did to his chest. "I've been," he cleared his throat of the lump, and started again. "I've been thinking about names."

"And?"

His throat closed up all over again. He imagined it would happen when he least expected for the next fifty or sixty years. She was so beautiful, artful and serene, her face pale against the soft pink robe. "How would you feel if we called him Storm?" he asked.

The baby moved, making another sound, making Sky and Meredith both grin. "Storm." She said it slowly, thoughtfully, as if testing it on her tongue. "Storm," she said again, stronger, more sure. "Storm Buchanan, I do believe your daddy would like to hold you."

Sky's breathing hitched, his gaze holding hers. The pupils of her eyes were dilated in the near darkness of pre-dawn, so that only a ring of brown encircled them. She was beautiful in a way he'd never seen before.

He'd held the baby shortly after he'd been born, but Sky was far from good at it. It took a little finagling to transfer the baby from her arms to his. Little Storm started to cry at having his world shifted, a lusty, healthy, awe-inspiring cry if there ever was one. He quieted as soon as he felt secure again in Sky's arms.

"He knows I'm his father."

Meredith nodded. "From the sounds of things, everybody knows."

They shared a telling look, before sharing a heartfelt smile. "How did they know?" she asked.

Sky answered, "Jake says that Josie said that the more

you started to show, the less I raced the wind after midnight. She's right, you know. I finally stopped running away from something, and started running toward you.''

Emotions welled in Meredith's heart. Any second now, tears were going to spill down her face.

''I was a fool not to believe you all along, Meredith. I'll never doubt your word again. How soon can you marry me?''

His voice had dipped so low she could almost feel the vibration of emotion along her sensitive skin. The intensity in his voice and in his eyes brought the tears spilling over her lashes. That intensity reached inside her, spreading to a place beyond her heart, to a place she couldn't name. She felt a curious sense of déjà vu, and yet she knew she'd never experienced anything like this, had never felt this way, had never loved or been loved like this. She'd never felt so full, so happy, so...tired.

''Very soon.'' She placed a hand along the baby's little body. The other hand, she placed along Sky's jaw.

She fell asleep that way, just drifted off. Sky watched her for a long time, amazed, and shaken. ''I'll be darned,'' he whispered to his son. ''Your mama really can smile in her sleep.''

He rocked the baby back and forth the way he'd seen Meredith do it. Storm Buchanan seemed like a lot of name for a six-pounder. But he was healthy, with wispy dark hair, round little cheeks and a strong grip for someone so small. It was a strong name, one he would grow into in time.

Sky had a lot of plans. He'd had lousy role models when he was growing up, but he would learn how to be the best father this beautiful, innocent child could ask for. He and Meredith had a lot of things to discuss. Wedding plans, for one thing. Sky had been thinking about taking over managing the feed store in town. He'd be close to Meredith while she worked at Hidden Treasures. He wanted to buy a house, too. He knew just who should decorate it. He didn't care where he lived, in town or in the country, as long as the three of them were together.

The baby made a mewling sound again. Meredith made an answering sound in her sleep. Being careful not to disturb her, he slid from the bed and strode around to the other side where there was more room. He settled next to Meredith just as the sun peeked over the horizon. It was New Year's Day, the beginning of a new year, a new life. Holding his son, sitting next to the woman he loved, he watched the sky turn lavender, pink, and blue. He loved, the woman and the child with a fierceness he'd never known was possible. It was an amazing morning, an amazing day, an amazing life. All because he'd met a woman one stormy night. Not just any woman, but the mother of the child they'd conceived that night.

Sky moved the baby to his shoulder. Everything he'd ever wanted was in this room. Leaning back against the pillows, he closed his eyes and tried to take it all in. He, Skyler Buchanan, had a family. He planned to spend the next hundred years being thankful.

Sky never heard the reporter enter the hospital room. He never saw the flash of her camera. But the following day, he and Meredith and the baby were on the front page of the local newspaper. The headline read, First Baby of the Year Arrives During Raging Storm. The caption below the photo of the three of them sleeping, read, "Sky Buchanan's Pride And Joy."

The article began with the words, "It seems another of those Jasper Gents has met the woman of his dreams. Just look at the smiles on their faces. The baby, a boy weighing in at six pounds even, arrived a month early in order to be the first baby born in the new year. His mother, Meredith, owns and operates Hidden Treasures, Antiques and Fine Furnishings in downtown Jasper Gulch. Apparently, the advertisement the local boys placed in the papers a few years back is still working. If any of you women out there are still waiting to meet the man of your dreams, there are still sixty bachelors in Jasper Gulch, and only a handful of marriageable women. It's a brand new year. As you can see from the photo, sometimes, dreams can and do come true."

*   *   *   *   *

Sandra Steffen has more
BACHELOR GULCH
books on the horizon.

Watch for Nathan Quinn's story,
available in May 2001
from Silhouette Romance.

This Valentine's Day, fall in love with men you can tell your mother about!

Silhouette Romance introduces Cody, Alex and Jack, three men who make pulses pound and hearts race.

Make them a Valentine's Day gift to yourself!

BE MY BRIDE? by Karen Rose Smith
(SR#1492)

Sexy Cody Granger returns to his hometown, little girl in tow, proposing a marriage of convenience to Lauren MacMillan. Dare Lauren accept the loveless bargain?

SECRET INGREDIENT: LOVE by Teresa Southwick
(SR#1495)

Can intense businessman Alex Marchetti tempt chef Fran Carlino to whip up something especially enticing for two...?

JUST ONE KISS by Carla Cassidy
(SR#1496)

Little Nathaniel's impulsiveness gave Jack Coffey a broken leg. Would his lovely mother, Marissa Criswell, do even more damage to his heart?

Available at your favorite retail outlet.

If you enjoyed what you just read,
then we've got an offer you can't resist!

Take 2 bestselling
love stories FREE!

Plus get a FREE surprise gift!

SILHOUETTE *Romance*

COMING NEXT MONTH

#1492 BE MY BRIDE?—Karen Rose Smith

Lauren MacMillan had never forgotten sexy Cody Granger. Then he returned to town, proposing a marriage of convenience to keep custody of his little girl. Dare Lauren trust Cody with the heart he had broken once before?

#1493 THE MESMERIZING MR. CARLYLE—Arlene James
An Older Man

He'd swept into her life, a handsome, charming, *wealthy* seafarer. But struggling single gal Amber Presley had no time for romance, though the mesmerizing Mr. Reece Carlyle seemed determined to make her his woman. Then she learned his secret motives....

#1494 TEX'S EXASPERATING HEIRESS—Carolyn Zane
The Brubaker Brides

She'd inherited a pig! And Charlotte Beauchamp hadn't a clue how to tame her beastly charge. Luckily, behaviorist Tex Brubaker sprang to her rescue. But his ultimate price wasn't something Charlotte was sure she could pay....

#1495 SECRET INGREDIENT: LOVE—Teresa Southwick

Businessman Alex Marchetti needed a chef, but was reluctant to hire beautiful and talented Fran Carlino. They'd both been hurt before in love, but their chemistry was undeniable. Could a confirmed bachelor and a marriage-shy lady find love and happiness together?

#1496 JUST ONE KISS—Carla Cassidy

Private investigator Jack Coffey claimed he was not looking for a family, but when he collided with little Nathaniel, he found one! As single mother Marissa Criswell nursed the dashing and surly man back onto his feet, she looked beyond his brooding exterior and tempted him to give her just one kiss....

#1497 THE RUNAWAY PRINCESS—Patricia Forsythe

Princess Alexis of Inbourg thought she'd found the perfect escape from her matchmaking father. But once she arrived in Sleepy River, she realized rancher—and boss!—Jace McTaggart was from a very different world. Would the princess leave her castle for a new realm—one in Jace's arms...?

CMN1200